FEEDING LUCY

FEEDING LUCY

A NOVELLA

MO MEDUSA

Feeding Lucy
© 2024 by Mo Medusa
All Rights Reserved.

No part of this publication may be reproduced, distributed, or transmitted in any form or by any means, including photocopying, recording, or other electronic or mechanical methods, without the prior written permission of the publisher, except as permitted by U.S. copyright law.

The story, all names, characters, and incidents portrayed in this production are fictitious. No identification with actual persons (living or deceased), places, buildings, and products is intended or should be inferred.

Published by Crooked Foot Press

ISBN-13:979-8-9913606-0-9 (paperback 1)
ISBN-13:979-8-9913606-2-3 (paperback 2)
ISBN-13:979-8-9913606-1-6 (eBook)

Cover Design by Christy Aldridge at Grim Poppy Designs

Edited by Nico Bell

Formatted by Joey Powell at Mad Axe Media

Printed in the United States of America
First edition

Instagram: @momedusahorror
Email: feedinglucybook@gmail.com

To Stella

SANKTA LUCIA

December 13th, 1975

Melted wax warmed my frozen fingers, dripping onto my skin as I waited patiently in line outside of the old church. A dozen other girls stood with me in the stone courtyard, all wearing white dresses with red sashes around our waists and holding singular white candles in our hands. We watched for our cue in the freezing cold, soft December snow falling from the night sky like glitter. A nun waved us on, prompting an older girl in front to lead the procession into the church, donning a pine tree crown affixed with large white candles cradling her perfect white-blonde curls.

I imagined her fiery crown catching a stray hair, setting the girl's head ablaze and wreaking havoc on the old cathedral. Churchgoers would rush from their pews, running for their lives as the building burned in the black sky. The ghosts would haunt us every December as the memories of that one disastrous night lived on for eternity. The town of Kolbe would never be the same again.

Hundreds of more candles illuminated the cathedral, the dancing flickers of light casting shadows on the ceiling and reflecting off the stained glass, creating colorful patterns across the massive church walls. Our red ribbons glowed with the flames as we assembled in the nave, organ blaring to prepare us for our performance of traditional Sankta Lucia songs.

Hark! Through the darksome night,
Sounds come a winging.
Lo! Tis the Queen of Light,
Joyfully singing.
Clad in her garment white,
Wearing her crown of light.
Sankta Lucia
Sankta Lucia.

My mother sat in the pew directly in front, waving her fingers around like an amateur orchestra conductor, her golden eyes piercing through me as she mouthed the words, making sure I wouldn't forget. Her yellow hair curled behind her ears, tucked neatly with pins that matched her shade perfectly. Her signature red lip slicked with gloss sparkled like the snow outside. She looked the most incredible I had ever seen her look.

The music was meant to be uplifting, but it felt cold, dark like the sky above. My lips sang the words, but my mind floated off into the air as I watched the snowfall doubling through the high windows, picking up faster and faster until I could only see piercing white through the tinted glass. Blizzards always made me uneasy, like the abundance of snow was a sign of something more sinister—a potion of evil being stirred in the night.

The big wooden doors shook in the wind, adding a natural percussion to the joyous singing. I thought the entire building might be trembling for a moment, but it must have just been the vibrations from the organs. The mighty wooden beams that floated across the pointed ceiling stayed firm, holding together hundreds of years of wood, plaster, and stone. I imagined what it would look like if all the fire from the candles burned out, leaving the cathedral cold and dark and the churchgoers scrambling to find their way out in the ever-growing snow outside.

But the flames still flickered, and the chorus continued singing, until three acolytes came out from the back room wearing white robes and holding brass bells with long handles to carefully snuff out the flames. When the last acolyte put out the last candle, the church went completely black, for just a second, until an usher or a volunteer turned the overhead lights back on and the priest gave his blessings before ending the service.

When we had said all our goodbyes and my mother had stuffed as much saffron bread and ginger biscuits into her purse as humanly possible, we walked home through the ferocious wind and sleet, down windy roads that brought us back to our humble little farmhouse in the middle of nowhere.

The mountain tops peaking in the misty distance looked like sharp claws reaching up from the depths of the earth. Crows cawed from the tops of trees, warning their friends and family that it was time to evacuate to safety. I imagined their cawing as witches cackling in the sky, flying around on broomsticks and casting spells on the innocent townsfolk below. My knees quivered at the thought.

We arrived home just as the wind picked up and even more snow fell to the ground. In the ten minutes that it took to arrive home, we didn't speak a word. I knew this meant my mother was disappointed in my performance that evening. I was lost in my own thoughts. Tempted by my imagination. I didn't pay enough attention, and now I was being punished by aching silence.

My mother jiggled the keys in the rusted lock, pushing her shoulder against the old heavy door. But without any additional force from my mother, the gusts blew the front door open, allowing us swift entry into our home before slamming shut again behind us.

My mother's cat, Zula, greeted us at the doorway, her scraggly gray fur falling off in chunks as she aged. She rubbed her head against my mother's leg, purring like a go-kart as my mother scratched her tiny head. She had been around since my mother was a child herself, and in her old age, the cat only trusted one person—Mama. I once tried to pet her, and she took a bite out of my hand so big it didn't heal for months. But it seemed my mother loved her more than she even loved me, so there was no use complaining to my mother any time Zula hissed, growled, or broke my skin apart 'til it bled. I tried to make nice and just leave her alone altogether.

Taking off my shiny tippy tappy shoes and shaking the heaps of snow from my shoulders onto the rug in the entryway, I looked up at my mother for approval and saw she looked sad, disappointed even.

"What's wrong, Mama?" I held onto her leg and pressed my head against her hip. I was worried I'd upset her. Upsetting her was my worst nightmare, an inevitable fate but one that I'd avoid at all costs.

"*Franciska*." The first word she'd spoken since we left the church. You have to remember to pay attention." My mother wisped away the fly away hairs in my face, tucking my light brown locks behind my ear. She sighed as she bent over and put her hands firmly on my shoulders, blowing her hot breath inches away from my face. "Little girls shouldn't have their heads in the clouds. They should *always* pay attention."

"Okay, Mama."

"Now get upstairs and into bed. And don't you *dare* think of throwing that beautiful dress on the floor to wrinkle and rot!"

"*Okay*, Mama."

I made sure to stomp extra loudly up the carpeted steps. I hated when she talked to me like a little kid.

Upstairs in my bedroom, I raced to rip the stuffy white dress off my body, throwing it on the floor in spite of my mother, and changing into a more comfortable plaid pajama set I found at the bottom of my drawer. I jumped in the bed, exhausted from my forced night at church, but still I wrestled with my knit comforter, unable to sleep with the harsh wind rattling the windows in their rusted frames and hitting the bare winter tree branches against the frozen glass. The hills of snow outside were so white they created a shining light that blared into my room, burning my eyes even when I tried to keep them closed.

The barren tree branches reminded me of long claws grasping at my windows, trying to get in and scratch me up into little slivers. The whistling wind sounded like werewolves howling at the moon, and the burning reflection from the growing snow piles was like white flames threatening to burn me for my sins. I sat up in bed, rubbing my eyes, when I heard my mother from downstairs. I tip-toed to the cracked bedroom door to listen better, creaking wooden floors threatening to blow my cover.

"Forgive me, Roland," she said, her tone hushed. She must have been on the telephone, but who was Roland? She kept talking to the mystery person, whispering in an accent I only heard come out when she was speaking to my grandmother in Polish. "I'm losing my grasp on her, she isn't listening to me like she used to."

Is she talking about me?

"Just give me more time with her. It won't be forever, I promise."

NEXT OF KIN

My blood vessels tightened in my forearms as I chugged another plastic cup of the spiked punch. The holiday party at work had been going on for at least an hour, enough time to get completely obliterated while trying to avoid hearing the same three Christmas songs played over and over. The annual holiday party was all anyone at the magazine could talk about for weeks before the event, mostly because it was an excuse to get drunk at work. My coworkers took turns screaming their favorite Christmas songs off-key during karaoke and exchanging presents. I thought it was stupid, a waste of a day. We could have been working instead or at least getting drunk in our own homes. But I participated as much as my introverted brain would let me, downing as much punch as my stomach would allow, hoping to make the party less miserable.

While my coworkers were busy gossiping and spilling their drinks on each other's shoes, I snuck to a lonely chair in a lonely corner—the perfect spot for someone who wanted nothing to do with anybody in the room. My head started to spin a bit, and I couldn't tell if it was because of the alcohol or the pounds of sugar my secretary liked to add to the punch. I put my head between my knees so I wouldn't puke from the spinning ceiling but that just made the floor spin, too. I closed my eyes and took a deep breath, trying to hold it together, but was interrupted by someone tapping on my shoulder with a long fingernail.

"Frankie," I heard my secretary say without looking up to see it was her. "Someone's on the phone for you, it sounds important."

"Fine."

I swallowed the bit of vomit that had formed in my throat and held onto the wall to stabilize myself while getting up from the chair. Who would be calling right *now?* It was nearly 8:30 p.m., way past closing time for the front desk. But I stumbled to my office anyway and fell into the green leather chair to answer the blinking phone.

"This is Frankie Bosko," I said, trying to hide the inebriation in my voice. I always sounded a little like my mother when I drank too much. "How can I help you?"

"Oh, my apologies," a man said. His voice sounded Slavic, maybe even Polish. "I was looking for someone named *Franciska.*"

"That's me," I sighed. "May I ask who's calling?"

"This is Mr. Ostrowski with the Kolbe Morgue," he said enthusiastically, like it was his favorite part of the job. I hadn't heard the name Kolbe in years, a town I thought I had forgotten, or at least tried to. "I'm afraid to inform you that a body was brought in today that seems to be your mother, Mrs. ... let's see here ... Lucja Bosko. That is your mother, correct?"

"Yes," I said with a groan. I hadn't spoken to my mother in ten years, and the first I heard of her since moving to the big city was to find out she was dead. What kind of sick joke was she playing on me? I wanted nothing to do with it—nothing to do with her. "Yes, that's my mother."

"We'll need you to come down and take care of her—"

"Oh no," I said, "I haven't been to Kolbe in a decade, and I don't plan on coming any time soon. Isn't there someone else who can deal with this?"

"Well, Miss Bosko," his voice changed from enthusiastic to persuasive. Like a car salesman who was about to lose his big commission if he didn't act now. "You *are* the only living relative, after all. Next of kin, and all that. You understand, don't you?"

"Sir, my mother was a miserable woman. If I never heard her name again, I'd be a happy woman."

"Well, I certainly understand your dilemma then, Miss Bosko." His voice now changed from persuasive to disappointed. The salesman was losing his big sale. "But if I may be frank, I don't believe that's the way a lady should speak. You were her only daughter, after all. I don't mean to impose, and I apologize if I come off a little harsh. But I have a sneaking suspicion you'd regret not seeing your mother one last time, paying your respects, and all. From the looks of it, you were all she had left. And besides, there is, of course, the whole matter of the estate."

I ignored the man's subtle digs at my womanhood—brushed off his entitlement to my emotions regarding my mother.

"Estate?" I asked, more alert than ever, now. The word stuck to my tongue and stayed there a while, lingering. I hadn't ever heard of my mother having an estate. Growing up I had always assumed we were poor, barely comfortable in our humble farmhouse. I never expected anything from my mother, and I certainly didn't expect anything after her death. "I didn't realize there was one."

"Why yes, of course!" Mr. Ostrowski's voice brightened to an enthusiastic tone again. "There's the house of course, and everything in it, and the most important part—the will. Seems you're getting a pretty penny, young lady."

I snuck out the back alley-side door after hanging up with the man on the phone. I avoided my drunk coworkers as they sloshed their drinks while shouting into the karaoke mic, taking extra precaution to not run into my boss, the editor in chief at the magazine. He always bombarded me with last minute projects that obliterated my weekend plans, and I always allowed it. Not this time.

The black city slush on my walk home seeped into my loafers, making a squishing noise in my shoes with each step, and then traveling up the runs in my pantyhose. The wind was biting, but the air felt clear, refreshing. It was like I could breathe fully for the first time.

The stone steps of my brownstone were covered in gushy melting snow, but I wasn't yet ready to leave the freedom of the outside world for the stuffiness of my apartment, even though my bladder screamed for relief. I brushed the wet snow off the top step and sat in the wetness, protected by my long puffer jacket. I sat on my front stoop for a while, reminiscing about my hometown and a life long ago.

"What business do you have going off on your own?" My mother ripped the suitcase from my hands, holding it hostage. "You're just a child, Franciska. A naive, stupid little child. You don't know what it's like in the city, the dangers that live in those streets, or all the strange men who are out for blood; out to get little girls like you. You wouldn't last a second out there!"

"I don't think you know a thing about me, Mom." I grabbed the handle of my suitcase and pulled until her fingers couldn't hold on any longer, setting it free from her grip. "Not everybody thinks the way you do."

My mother laughed, placing her hand on her hip and scanning me up and down with her eyes.

"Just look at you." Her mouth turned down in disgust. "Your shabby loose clothing and long, unkempt hair. You look like one of those ... one of those ..."

"If you're going to say it, just say it." I started to walk away, but the courage I'd never had before suddenly found itself resting in my gut. "Think whatever you want about me. Maybe you're right."

"Well, aren't you proud of yourself?" my mother said, following me down the hall to the front door. "You must think you're so much better than everybody here in Kolbe, don't you? Like you got it all figured out. But you don't even know who you are! I tried with you, Franciska, I really did. Since the day you were born, I tried to show you the beauty of our traditions, but you always rejected it. Even as a little girl you were uninterested, and as you grew older it only got worse. And now you've resorted to insulting our culture altogether! You're a selfish little girl, barely an adult for one week, and you already think you know better than the person that raised you!"

"Like I've told you, Mom," I said, fighting the tears welling in my eyes, "I'm just not like you."

Walking through the front door felt like walking into a new world, away from it all. The fear that crumbled my bones dissipated more with every step further from my childhood home.

The taxi I'd ordered was already waiting for me a few feet down the road, and I hurried through the muddy grass to catch it before the driver left. But I stopped for a moment when my mother's voice echoed through the wind from the front porch.

"You won't be gone for long," she shouted. "I promise you that!"

My bladder throbbed, interrupting the stream of tears gushing from my face. Wiping my eyes with my jacket sleeve, I stumbled while getting up from the steps, drunker than I thought. I *really* had to pee by the time I made it up to my third-floor apartment, squeezing my legs together while I struggled to get the key in the door. Just as my bladder was about to explode and release urine all over the new hallway rugs, the key turned and the door flew open, allowing me sweet release in the comfort of my tiny bathroom.

Packing to meet my dead mother proved to be chaotic as always. I grabbed whatever I could find that wasn't dirty or crumpled into a ball on the floor and stuffed it into an old high school soccer duffel I found in the back of my closet. I didn't know how long I'd be back home in Kolbe, but I cleaned out my drawers full of t-shirts and jeans, packing heavy just in case.

The band shirts from concerts past were in abundance, practically the only pieces of clothing I owned. Everything looked the same—black and worn—until I came across a baby blue floral blouse with ruffles in the front and a scrunched up bustier, a relic from my days of trying to appease my mother with obscene femininity. The soft tulle fabric melted at my fingertips, wisping me off to the past again. I sat on the floor in a pile of wrinkled clothing, but my mind was in a different place.

"Keep this to remember me by," she said, handing me her favorite blouse from her closet—the one she wore to almost every special occasion, the one I'd seen her wearing six months ago when we first met. Her wide smile showed all her white teeth in one perfect picture, a cruel sight to have to walk away from.

"I'll treasure it," I said with a half-smile, fighting back tears and trying to look as attractive as I'd hoped she'd always remember me. "But I wish you could come with me."

"I wish I could too."

We embraced, my hands finding their way through her thick raven hair, weaving themselves between the strands and holding on tightly. She smelled like heaven and fruit trees, an intoxicating combination that wafted through my nostrils and sunk deep into my chest. I'd never forget that smell as long as I lived.

"It's not fair." I sobbed onto her shoulder, longing for the part of me that was soon to be missing.

"I have an idea," she said, pulling away from me to look for something in her bedroom. She grabbed a small razor from her closet shelf, presenting it to me like it was a prize before placing it in my palm. "I know a way we can stay close to each other, even from afar."

I looked at her like she spoke a strange new language that hadn't existed before.

"What is this, a blood oath or something?"

"Something like that." She giggled and my heart almost burst. Her laugh was what drew me to her the first time we met six months before, and it was what kept me around even when she came up with wild ideas involving razors.

"I don't know, Stell."

"It won't hurt, I promise." She took the razor from my hand, and as carefully as ever, sliced a small line into her palm, sealing it with a kiss. Looking up to me with her enchanting yellow eyes, she gently grabbed my hand, slicing another line into my palm, kissing it with her plump lips. "There. Now we're connected for life."

I kissed her one last time, not even minding the coppery taste of blood that had mixed with her shimmery lip balm, leaving its trace behind. I wanted to keep the taste on my lips as long as I could.

Still in the pile of unfolded band t-shirts, I found myself rubbing the palm of my left hand, right where a tiny scar used to be, now faded away with time. I hadn't noticed an entire hour go by as I sat on the wood floors of my bedroom.

Stuffing the pile of shirts into my duffel and zipping it up, I collapsed into bed, curling up into my down comforter as the wind whistled outside my window.

I fell asleep dreaming about the girl who got away.

INTO THE MOUNTAINS

I slept only a few hours, leaving before the crack of dawn. I brought every Pixies tape I owned to accompany me on my four-hour drive from the city back home to the Kolbe country. I popped *Trompe le Monde* in my cassette player, turning the volume up as loud as it would go, turning the key and letting the Bronco rumble a bit before shifting to *drive* and pressing the gas.

I decided I was going to try to make it all the way to Kolbe without stopping. No food stops, no detours, not even a pee break. The plan was to stay only one night at my mother's house—identify the body, sign the will, get my money and *go*. I didn't plan on sticking around the place that had proved over and over again that I wasn't welcome. *A girl like me* had no place in a small, lonely town like that. I hadn't planned on going there ever again. But in order for Kolbe to really be behind me for good, I had to just get it over with.

The city sparkled in the night, the lights on the skyscrapers bright enough to see from space, or at least that's what I imagined. I pictured all the wealthy families in their high-rise apartments, looking down on the massive urban utopia. The lake reflected the sparkling buildings like a mirror, the entire skyline blasted on the frozen winter water. But the farther south I drove, the less sparkly buildings I saw and the more dilapidated old homes, empty lots covered in broken beer bottles and other garbage.

Even further south and all I saw were hills of dead winter grass; barren cornfields covered in snow that had surely turned to ice by now. The drive turned from flat city streets to large hilly roads, with the peaks of mountains creeping in closer and closer from the foggy distance.

A hundred miles south into the middle of tight mountain roads and nowhere, I found myself lost in the vast snowy peaks of the blue-ridged Babia Mountains. The sun was fully erect now but hiding behind black clouds and opaque mist. It still looked like nighttime, although according to the clock on my car stereo, it was already 9 a.m. I turned on the brights of my Bronco, but I still couldn't see more than a foot in front of me. The snow had started to pick up, faster than I had expected. The flurries flew fast, like frosted waves blasting from a tsunami. The size of the snowflakes astounded me; they were as large as my fist, something I'd never seen. The intricate crystal webs fell on my windshield like exploding boulders, hitting the glass and blowing apart into a confetti cannon of frigid white powder.

The windshield wipers on my old Bronco weren't strong enough to keep the snow from covering my view completely, and my defroster stopped working nearly twenty miles up the mountain. I looked at the gas meter—I only had another fifty miles before I was shit out of luck, stuck in a blizzard in the middle of nowhere. I was completely lost, barely able to see the dirt road in the fog and snow, and running out of fuel, without a gas station in sight.

Fuck, I thought, knowing I had at least another forty miles before I was in Kolbe, and there was no way to call for help. I hadn't seen another person—another living thing—since leaving city limits. I was out in the wilderness all alone, just me, my Bronco, and my Pixies tapes. It didn't help that the small dirt roads twisted and turned, winding around peaks and flying high over valleys miles below. I was terrified of driving in these parts after having the luxury of living in a large city for the last decade.

I wasn't used to the slippery muddiness of unpaved roads any longer. I hadn't seen snow like this in years, even in the dead of winter. I was in a mess of culture shock, but the culture was the natural environment surrounding me. I drove carefully down the slippery roads, traveling at less than five miles per hour the entire time. The mountain peaks were unforgiving, looming over me and my truck at every turn, reminding me of the dark pointed edges that prey on unsuspecting hikers or animals who have lost their way. I hadn't ever climbed those mountains or even dared think about it.

Ten more miles passed before the snow calmed. I was back to driving at a normal speed, finally inching toward Kolbe—toward the money and being done with my mother for good. But after driving so slowly for so long, I was making horrible time, already more than four hours in with over thirty miles left to travel. But with determination and a hunger for the *pretty penny* I was about to receive, (and the Polish food I'd be submerged in when I got there) I focused on the road. Nothing but the road. The dark and frosted road to home and back to my mother.

It was like she was in the car with me, sitting in the passenger seat, smiling bright and happy because I'd finally decided to come home. The hairs on my wrists swayed with the memory of her softly rubbing my forearms at night when I was a child, soothing me to sleep. In the cold winters she'd bring me an extra knit blanket, usually one she'd made herself, wrapping it around the two of us until I drifted off to dreamland, and she'd leave me curled up in the blanket, still feeling her warmth on my skin.

"One day you'll learn how to knit your own blanket for your own family," she'd always say.

But oh, how little my mother knew about me.

I breathed in a deep yawn, only then realizing how long the trip had been. My eyelids fluttered in exhaustion, and my head pounded from the spiked punch the night before. My fingertips and toes tingled as the poison made its way through my body; my organs begging for clean hydration. The road in front of me blurred as the bright light from the snow started to seep through the slits in my eyes, but the lower my eyelids sank, the darker the road became, darker and colder until it was black, blacker than the clouds in the sky. Mom was sitting next to me again, gently caressing the hairs on my arms, wrapping a colorful knit blanket around the two of us, until I drifted off ...

I awoke only a few feet down the road, startled by my own gasping and the Bronco crashing into a snow-covered bush. I jumped out of the truck to investigate any damages, nearly slipping to my death as I hopped down from the driver's seat before realizing the vehicle was inches away from the edge of the mountain. I did a quick scan of the front of the truck—no damages save for a few scratches from the sharp winter bushes. But a quiet rumbling coming from underneath the car made me investigate further, worried I'd unintentionally collected some roadkill on my trip home.

I looked into the dark underbelly of the massive monstrosity of a vehicle and saw nothing, but when I kicked the side of the old truck, something small and dirty-looking scurried away. I stood up, searching for the animal, dying to know what sort of creature was due to meet its fate on the roads of the Babia mountains. I looked into the white blanketed distance and saw nothing but stopped when I felt a tug at the bottom of my jeans. A small cat was pawing at my ankles, skinny, disheveled, and dirty from his unfortunate life in the Babias.

"Get off of me!" I yelled, my voice echoing through the vast mountaintops. I shook my ankle and the cat's skinny body flew a foot or two into the snowy road. I thought I'd killed it, and the guilt instantly set in. "I'm so sorry ... oh, my god, I'm so sorry!"

But before I could start to blame myself for all the world's problems—including the murder of an innocent cat—the animal got up again and just stood there, staring at me, showing its sharp teeth and growling with a high-pitched rumble from the depths of its empty stomach. The cat's final warning was a loud hiss, flashing its teeth again before running away into the frozen mountain forest. My heart pounded through my chest and my breath was quick and shallow, but at least I was no longer at risk of falling asleep.

Back in the Bronco, I popped another Pixies tape—*Doolittle*—into the cassette player and pressed play, leaving the volume at full blast and letting the music assist me in the final stretch back to Kolbe. But when the album got to track number seven, "Monkey Gone to Heaven," the song skipped, and the ribbons of magnetic tape started flying out of the cassette player.

"Fuck!" I yelled, trying to collect all of the tape that piled on top of itself on the truck floor. I pressed *eject* on the stereo and pulled the cassette out, hoping I could salvage it later, but the tape had ripped in half at the spindles and the plastic was cracked. "How the hell did this happen?"

Frustrated, I switched the dial on the car stereo to FM radio, hoping to find a weather channel that actually got reception in the mountains. Although it was December, the blizzards made of giant snowflakes seemed unnatural for this point in the season. It had been a long time since I'd been up in the Babia Mountains, but not that long. I knew that the big snowstorms out there didn't typically get bad until after Christmas when the whole town shut down to outsiders. The rest of the winter season was always frozen solid, unmoving for months.

I flipped through various country stations and channels full of just static until I found the lone weather reporting out there in the middle of nowhere. The meteorologist spoke quickly and with urgency like he was delivering important news, although his message was unclear. The man's voice went in and out, blasting loud crackling into the truck every other word, sometimes in the middle of a word. I could barely make out what he was saying.

"The ... blizz ..." He sounded like he was in the middle of the storm itself. "Unusual storms ..." his voice cut off again. It was useless; the farther I drove into the mountains, the more interference replaced the man speaking and cut me off from any information about the brewing storms. The static from the radio whooshed like the wind outside, but more cutting, sharp. I was about to turn the volume down altogether when the meteorologist's voice came through clearly.

"If you're planning on spending a remote holiday in the Babia Mountains, turn around now. The National Weather Service urges everyone to stay home this Christmas. I repeat: Go home *now*."

KOLBE

I arrived in Kolbe with an empty stomach and mere miles to spare on the gas meter. Driving through the mountains again was like driving through a ghost town; the people's faces on the street seemed distant and unfamiliar. The children walking with their parents in hand weren't children I had known when I was young, but a new generation of Kolbe townsfolk, destined to either be stuck there forever, or run away from it all as soon as they got a chance, never to look back.

The moving clouds slipped through the dark spots in the sky, appearing in fragmented bursts as a quick spotlight on the small town. The colorful Christmas lights twinkled on the sides of the old European-style buildings, bringing glimpses of joy to a dark and cold winter. The Polish-Catholic church in the center of town stood strong atop the giant hills of Kolbe, looming over the small city, reminding the townsfolk of their heritage.

The red poppies that appeared every spring were planted by my mother every fall. Their green stalks fought hard to stay alive through the cold, preparing themselves for their blooms even through the winter. I could see the little green sprouts of life poking through the dead grass and snow, begging for warm sun. Her fingers had touched every inch of this place, her influence in the town apparent even a decade after I'd left. In Kolbe, I couldn't pretend my mother didn't exist.

I finally stopped driving when the growling in my stomach brought me to a place I thought I'd forgotten—the Kolbe Diner. My favorite spot to clear my head as a teenager, the Kolbe Diner was the best place to get half-frozen french fries, burgers that tasted like grease-trap, and the best milkshakes imaginable. Walking into the restaurant felt like coming home for the first time.

Bells jingled as I opened the glass diner door, startling a middle-aged waitress who was sitting in a booth with her feet up, reading a tabloid magazine. Her glasses lowered when the bells rang, alerting her of the only customer in the building. She seemed to be there all by herself.

"I'll be with you in a minute, sweetheart!" she called to me, still under her magazine and using her red pointed fingernail to trace the words she was reading. Her large purple glasses sat right on the bridge of her nose, just below her eyes, attached with a beaded strap around her neck. When she finished learning the latest celebrity gossip, she placed the open magazine interior side down on the table, grabbed a menu from a bin next to her, and walked over to seat me.

"Just put me anywhere," I said, shuffling in place and trying not to make it obvious I was squeezing my legs together like a child about to pee their pants. "But can I use your washroom?"

"Sure, sweetheart," the waitress said, placing the menu on the closest table to her and pointing to a dark corner in the back of the diner. "It's back there."

I relieved myself of a day and a half's worth of punch and piss, watching it swirl down the hole in the toilet before zipping back up and washing my hands. The small bathroom sink looked ancient; it was cracked in two places and like it hadn't been cleaned in decades. The mirror that hung above the sink was covered in grime, blurring my reflection but not enough that I couldn't see my disheveled state. My eyes looked sunken and dark, like I hadn't slept in days. The veins in my neck looked swollen, about to burst. I looked closer at the dirty mirror, fixing the stray hairs that curled out of my ponytail, trying to look more presentable. But in the mirror my features started to shrink away, the round-ness of my cheeks sunk inward, revealing my cheekbones, and my skin turned gray. I focused more closely on my face, getting as close as I could without touching the mirror with my nose. The face staring back at me started to twist and turn until the features were out of place, the eyes darkening. I blinked and it had changed again. The face I saw now looked exactly like my mother, like I was staring *at* my mother. She smiled with sharp crooked teeth, and I jumped back, hitting my back into the paper towel dispenser.

I need to get some rest, I thought.

Shaking off whatever the hell had happened in the bathroom, I sat down at the table the waitress had prepared for me. She stood there waiting.

"Would you like to see the lunch specials?" she asked politely.

"No thank you," I said, still a little jittery. "I'll just take a coffee."

"No problem, sweetheart." Grabbing the pot off the countertop and pouring the hot brown liquid into my cup, the waitress looked at me like she pitied me, judging me in my sweaty travel attire. "What brings you to town?"

"Just business," I said, trying not to make conversation but failing to keep my mouth shut. "I grew up here."

"Is that right?" she exclaimed, her gray eyes brightening. "Well, I hope you're around in a few days for the big Sankta Lucia Day celebration. It's gonna be fabulous!"

The words *Sankta Lucia Day* rang familiar bells in my ears, but I couldn't remember exactly what they meant. "What's that?" I asked.

"You're tellin' me you grew up in Kolbe and you don't know about Sankta Lucia?" She shook her head in disbelief as she threw her order book on the table and sat down across from me at my booth. "That's impossible. You must have been in the procession as a little girl ..."

The waitress took her glasses off her face and let them hang from the beaded chain around her neck, resting on her name tag that read, *Jeannine*.

"I guess I just forgot the details," I said, putting my head down in shame. "Could you remind me?"

Jeannine's eyes brightened at the insistence that she tell me more about her favorite holiday. She boasted proudly about the old tradition of Sankta Lucia Day, what she called the festival of lights. A magical day according to her, it was meant to bring light to the darkening winter—a celebration of good ruling over evil, and all that crap. But her religious history lesson didn't even bother me as I sat there sipping the diner coffee that tasted like warm vinegar; it was nice to have company after way too many hours alone in the Bronco.

"It started in Sweden or one of those Scandinavian countries. Beautiful young girls in white dresses wear candle-lit Christmas wreaths on their heads, leading the procession through the dark night into the church that is lit by hundreds and hundreds of burning candles." Her cheeks blushed as she gushed over talks of the celebration. "It's a magical event, you have to come!"

"It sounds great," I said, still sipping my bitter coffee slowly. *And familiar,* I thought to myself. A faint image of girls in white dresses wearing candles on their heads flashed in my memory but was gone as soon as it came. I could only remember little bits of the town, like the greasy burgers at the diner, and a few memorable faces. But big celebrations like Sankta Lucia Day must have faded from my memory, like they simply disappeared. "But why does a Polish immigrant town care so much about a Scandinavian holiday?"

"Oh," said Jeannine, chuckling while standing back up to clean the counters. "You know how Catholics are with their Saints. They all start to become the same after a while. And besides, Kolbe gets so dark and dreary this time of year, it's nice to bring a little light back into town."

Outside the diner windows, the clouds deepened to a rich charcoal black as the day switched over from morning to afternoon. The darkest time of the year meant that the light in the sky would fully disappear before dinnertime, leaving the town an empty void of lifelessness. The Christmas lights that hung from the awnings of all the town's businesses glistened against the harsh blackening sky, warming the town with life. It was a perfect juxtaposition, the twinkling lights gleaming, only able to shine as bright as they were because the night was so stark black. Maybe I was being too judgmental before, and Sankta Lucia really was as special as the town and Jeannine claimed. Maybe the candles were more than just a special celebration of an honored saint, but *necessary*. A town like this—in the middle of nowhere, on top of a mountain, covered in ice and snow—can't survive without a little bit of light.

I took the last sip of my vinegar-coffee mixture, leaving a twenty on the table under the bowl of sugar cubes, even though that was far too much money for one cup of terrible coffee. Jeannine's company felt comfortable, a friendly face in the freezing cold mountain winter.

"Thanks for the coffee, Jeannine." I waved goodbye and pushed the glass door open, jingling the bells again. But before I got out the door, Jeannine started waddling toward me with her hands up.

"Wait!" she yelled, huffing as she tried to catch up with me. "Please say you'll come to Sankta Lucia Day. Bring your boyfriend if you want. I'm sure a pretty girl like you must have a *boyfriend*, right?"

"I'll think about it," I chuckled, knowing I was lying.

Older folks were always inquiring about some invisible boyfriend that only existed in their minds. It was like their brains couldn't comprehend that maybe I didn't like *boys* at all. And regardless of who I chose to spend my private time with, I had only planned to spend one night in Kolbe, and I wasn't going to stick around longer than I needed to—even for my new friend Jeannine. The festival of lights sounded nice for a small dark town like Kolbe, but I needed to get back home to the lights of the city, the ones that never turned off.

Jeannine smiled as I walked out of the diner, showing her brown, jagged teeth.

DESPERATE MEOWING

The white paint on the old farmhouse had nearly all chipped away, uncovering years of weathered shiplap. The porch sunk in a little in the middle, like the wood was rotting. My mother had just died a few days ago, but if I didn't know any better, I'd think the house was abandoned. The biting wind made the unlatched handle on the rusted mailbox spin around, scraping together metal on metal and making the most horrific screeching sound. The cold made my eardrums ache, and my bones harden into crisp icicles, ready to shatter into frosted dust. I didn't think I'd ever be back to my childhood home, having forgotten its rotting walls as soon as I stepped foot on land outside of the claustrophobic mountain hole of Kolbe. Standing on the sinking porch of the home I left long ago, I felt sick to my stomach.

Sticking my hand beneath the large flowerpot of hibernating poppies and dried out dirt, I grabbed the spare house key that I knew would be taped to the underneath. Mom hadn't changed a bit. I stuck the key into the lock, jiggling the doorknob a little before turning the key, just as I always did when I still lived with Mom. Apparently not all my memories of Kolbe were lost.

The heavy door creaked as I struggled to push it open past the vacuum of wind that formed through the house. My mother must have never gotten around to fixing the cracked window back in the kitchen. The house was silent, as expected, but still my gut ached like something wasn't quite right. My mother's things were splayed across the family room but in her meticulous way—a pencil never far from a notepad, a television remote stuffed in a couch cushion for easy access. To the average person it would seem the house was a mess, but my mother always knew where everything was, and moving any of her things meant trouble for whoever dared to try.

My mother being dead didn't stop my heart from pounding when I shoved a pile of her crap off the couch and plopped on the seat, exhausted. But I didn't fall into a soft cushion covered by a worn homemade throw. Instead, I fell onto another pile of something warm, something with bones, something breathing. I snapped my body behind me to see what I'd potentially crushed, and the thing sprinted away producing a high-pitched snarl. Glowing eyes from down the hall stared at me as I approached it, ready to catch whatever rodent had broken into the house in my mother's absence. But when I got closer, the creature made a familiar sound—it meowed.

"Zula?" I spoke at the creature, still unsure what I was looking at in the dark. But when I saw her ears perk up at the sound of her name, I knew I wasn't imagining things. "How the hell are you still alive?"

The cat's unbelievable age appeared in broken teeth and missing tufts of gray fur, only visible as she inched her slow body near my feet, producing raspy mews of pain with every step. She flopped on the floor at my ankles, and I thought her bones would all disintegrate as her fragile body hit the hardwood. I did the math in my head and calculated that Zula must have been at least forty years old, an impossible thing to believe even as I stared at the decrepit feline in front of me.

I imagined my mother casting a spell on the ancient cat, keeping her alive long beyond her years to comfort her in her loneliness. It was sad, really.

It didn't take long to hear the hunger in the old cat's desperate meowing, and her labored head tilts toward the back of the house indicated the food must have been in or near the kitchen. I followed behind Zula's calculated steps, being careful not to step on her ancient paws. I didn't know what sort of fate I'd meet for damaging the world's oldest living pet cat. I found the bag of *advanced-age* cat food in the cabinet under the sink, and two bowls conveniently placed on the floor next to it. I filled one with clean water, the other clearly meant for the kibble. I didn't know how much to feed her, so I just filled the bowl, enticing the elderly creature to slither like a snake headfirst toward the meal, inhaling the food like she hadn't eaten in months.

With nothing left to accomplish that night, I left the cat to enjoy her dinner and traipsed upstairs to pass out. Like habit, I turned left at the top stair to enter my childhood bedroom but found only stacks of boxes and no bed. When I was home my mother couldn't let me be, like her only job was to enforce her ever changing rules or obsess over whether I had broken something precious of hers. Everything I ever touched, created, or owned was meticulously inspected, either deemed worthy of displaying (but only in my bedroom) or thrown out in disgust. But knowing that she had decided to pack my entire life away—stuffing all my trophies and pictures and memorabilia into boxes and pretending I'd never existed—till tore into the hole in my gut that had always wished for her approval.

But when closing the door to shut away my past, something squishy and small fell from the dresser into the doorframe. A red velvet pouch with something fragrant inside fell at my feet, enticing me to open it. Looking inside, I found crumbles of dried herbs stuck to the velvet fabric, smelling of something familiar.

Is that oregano? I thought.

Finding it strange, I wondered why I would keep a bag full of seasoning in my room all those years. But I stuffed it into my jeans pocket anyway, my gut screaming that something about it was important. Shutting the door, I walked to the other end of the hallway.

The only other bed in the house was in my mother's bedroom, the last place I felt comfortable staying in. But with the only other option being a lumpy old couch and the hardwood floors, I didn't have a choice.

My mother's room was perfectly preserved, a time capsule of all the things she had loved in her life—an exhibit at the history museum dedicated to the late great Lucja "Lucy" Bosko. She would've loved the thought of that; being remembered—even for the bad things—was something she'd always dreamt of. Everything was always about my mother, my whole life constructed from bits and pieces of her life in Poland, a completely different world than I had ever known. Even this joke of a town was just a relic of her roots, a town built off the backs of immigrants, all from the same small city in Poland. A city that served as the blueprint for a strong but stubborn community of people who feared change; anything outside of what our ancestors did decades ago in a land thousands of miles away.

Even the trinkets and cosmetics and little glass bottles that were placed in organized chaos across her vanity were all pieces of Poland—traces of back home. I wanted to collect all of the oddly shaped and brightly colored vases and bowls in my hands and smash them on the hardwood, shattering Poland's *finest glass in the world* into a billion little pieces that could never be put back together. I didn't hate Poland itself, or even that my mother was born there. What I hated was that in this house, there couldn't ever be another way, a modern opinion, a love for anything other than the stupid fucking *Mountains in the Old Country*. I wanted to break it all apart, every memory, every thought, every piece of artistic glass that ever had a "made in Poland" sticker on the bottom.

And I did. In my anger, I didn't realize that I had swiped all my mother's things off of her vanity and onto the floor, spilling powders and creams and newly destroyed antiques. I panicked, like a child who'd done something she wasn't supposed to and now had to clean it up before her mother found out what I had done in my stupid, selfish, *inconsiderate little girl* anger. And yet, my heart still beat out of my eardrums like I was being chased by something dark, something evil, something living in my mother that only I had ever seen.

Faded crimson petals spread across the messy floor brought me out of the bowels of panic and into the happier pits of my memory. My mother, a creature of habit, still kept dried poppies on hand at all times, displaying them in a crystal bowl on her vanity after picking the petals from her endless supply around town. *You never know when you'll need them*—a sentiment driven into me by her design, a thought that forever stuck to the hidden parts of my memory.

I played with the velveteen petals as I picked them off of the floor one by one. They were only halfway dried on the curling edges, like my mother had recently picked them and was waiting before turning them into her famous "bedtime" tea. A concoction of poppies and other flowers and herbs, the tea and I spent many a night together, the liquid heat in my belly dusting my insides with hazy dream-coated tranquility.

Magic invisible powders left on the decaying poppy petals coated my fingertips as I continued to play with them, releasing their powers of slumber. My eyelids sunk over my dehydrated eyes, fluttering before locking in place. My body soon followed, my weakened limbs succumbing to the gravitational pull of the floor beneath me. Finally, I laid on the cold hardwood, curled up like a child in deep sleep. One last breath in and I was off to another place, dreaming with the poppies.

COLD BONES

The weathered gray brick that contained the Kolbe mortuary was covered in dark vines that twisted around corners, infiltrating continuous life into the cracks that formed on the house of the dead. The hills of brown grass behind the building held rows of stone grave markers, proudly presenting the names and memories of the decaying Kolbe townsfolk underneath. I walked the splintered steps to the front door, a heavy wooden monstrosity with a metal placard that read: *Roland Ostrowski: Kolbe County Mortician.*

The brass door knocker made an echoing boom as I hit the wooden door three times, unsure if I was allowed to walk in unannounced. After a moment of listening to the group of black crows that were huddled by a tree in the cemetery, staring at me, a short old man with a mean exaggerated frown swung the heavy door open, knocking me off balance and nearly pushing me off the porch.

"My apologies, miss!" The old man's angry face didn't match his demeanor. "These doors are tricky. Come in, come in! I'm Roland Ostrowski, the mortician here, and I assume you're Franciska?" His short stubby fingers waved me inside the dark metal-gray morgue.

"Please," I begged of him. "Call me *Frankie.*"

A chill that was colder than the winter air outside hit my skin like knives as I walked in— reminder of the bodies that lay there frozen in the walls, waiting to be put in their proper burial place, or burned to crumbled bone and ash. Mr. Ostrowski pointed to a folding chair in the small waiting area, instructing me to sit.

"Just wait right here while I get your documents prepared for signing. Stella here will take care of you in the meantime."

The name drew a knife through my belly, twisting my guts into a tangled blob.

It couldn't be, could it?

No, that's just silly. She must have left here years ago, like we'd always planned ...

But there behind a tall receptionists' desk sat the most beautiful woman I'd ever seen and one I never thought I would get to speak to again. The *one that got away*—my first love, and the girl I had to walk away from when I left Kolbe—was sitting right in front of me, looking more magnificent than in my dreams.

Dark curls wrapped around her face in perfect tendrils, stopping just at the nape of her neck. Her light-brown eyes with gold flecks in the middle sparkled against the harsh fluorescent lighting, glowing just as they always had. She was exactly as I had remembered her, but better; her skin bright with wisdom and a decade of life lived.

Her smile when she looked up to greet me warmed my veins even as I waited in the freezing reception area, grasping at the vessels in my pumping heart.

"Hi Frankie," Stella said, her voice now deeper than when we were teenagers—brassier. "It's really good to see you."

"Stella ..." Her name came out in a whisper, vocal cords shaky. "I can't believe it's really you."

"I can't believe it either," she said, getting up from her desk to bring me a cold bottle of Polish Spring water, our fingers gently brushing against each other's as she placed the bottle in my hand. She sat down next to me, and I could feel my pulse through my eyeballs. She was as cool as ever; I was a wreck of nerves. "I'm sorry about your mom. I know you two weren't close, but still, I know it must be difficult." As she got closer, the smell of fruit trees and heaven infiltrated my senses. "I ... I don't know if this is too much to say at a time like this but ... I've missed you. A lot."

In that mere second, I dreamed an entire dream that she had felt the same warmth in her veins as I had, exhibited the same obsession with the flecks of color in my eyes. I wondered if she'd ever thought about me all those years—imagining how things would be if I hadn't left.

"Did you ..." Anxiety crept in through shaky hands and thoughts of rejection. But her smile instilled in me a sense of confidence, and I went on. "Ever wish things were different?"

Stella giggled, sounding like her teenage self again.

"Not here. My uncle won't be long." She smiled again, pushing her hair behind her ears and quickly shifting her gaze to the floor. "He just needs a few minutes to get all the boring paperwork handled."

"The mortician is your uncle?" I asked. "I never knew that."

"Yes," she said, tucking her dark tendrils behind her ear. "My parents' health started to decline pretty quickly after you left, maybe even the second you drove away. It was strange, Frankie. Having to grieve my first love, all the while grieving my dying parents. They passed on the same day, mere months after I'd lost you, too. Uncle Roland took me in straight away, and I couldn't be more grateful for his help. He really got me through my sadness after their deaths, which I didn't think I'd ever make it out of. So, when he needed help here at the morgue a few years back, it wasn't even a question that needed to be asked. I started the very next day, and I never left."

"Oh, Stella ..." I leaned into her, our gazes meeting at last. "I'm so sorry. I feel terrible that I wasn't here for all that, that I wasn't here for you. I should've at least tried to call, or send a letter, or something. I shouldn't have left you the way I did, I shouldn't have—"

"Shhhh," she whispered, placing her moisturized pointer on my lips. "You couldn't possibly have known about any of this. And besides, that was so long ago. Now you're back and we can finally finish what we started..."

Just as we (at least in my imagination) were about to kiss, the back-office door creaked open and Mr. Ostrowski walked back into the waiting area, holding a stack of documents larger than my college thesis paper. Stella jumped out of her chair and shuffled back to her receptionist desk, obviously afraid of what her uncle might say or do. I didn't picture him a stern boss, but maybe he worked her to the bone. Or maybe she just didn't want him to see *us*.

"You can come back now, Franciska," he said with a jolly voice, still contradicting the mean mug he wore plastered to his face. Our moment was interrupted, lost to the realities of my circumstances. I didn't want to leave her, but I followed the man anyway.

But as I passed by her desk, I felt her baby-soft hand grab mine, placing a crumpled piece of paper in my palm. I quickly scanned the note behind Mr. Ostrowski's back.

Lunch later? –Xoxo, Stella

The note was completed with her phone number and a little smiley face at the end. I was hooked. I waved to her shyly—shivers traveling through my heart.

Mr. Ostrowski's office was smaller than a coat closet, with just enough room for a little desk and piles of dusty medical books, glass bottles of strange liquids, taxidermy birds clinging on to stick perches, and other oddities. A brass statue of a Polish eagle took up an entire corner of his desk, but he worked around it with ease. His messy office was in complete disarray, but it seemed he knew where everything was. Organized chaos, exactly like my mother.

"You just need to sign these forms here, giving the town consent to do what we will with the body," he said, shuffling through the stack of papers without looking up at me. His jolly demeanor from before hid behind the pile of documents, disappearing as his hard-at-work personality took over. "I will need to take you back to see her, if that's alright. The county makes us identify every body that comes through, if they have enough recognizable features left to identify them with, of course."

"Like her *dead* body?" I asked, realizing immediately how stupid that sounded. Of course he meant her dead body, I was sitting in a mortician's office at the morgue for Christ's sake. The idea that the first time I was seeing my mother in ten years just happened to be at a place like this, was kind of funny when I didn't think about it too hard. I tried not to think about anything too hard; all I wanted was to get out of there, out of that town. I dreamed of grabbing my bag of inherited money and rescuing Stella from her uncle's shabby mortuary, taking her back to my home in the city, and treating her like the queen she was. But I couldn't do anything like that until I was done identifying my mother's body and had the money in my hands. At that moment, all I had to do was answer the old man. "I mean yeah, I guess."

After sloppily signing the documents as quickly as possible and without even looking, I followed Mr. Ostrowski into the large room that held the metal mortuary chambers, storing frozen bodies like rows of pastries at a bakery. Mr. Ostrowski looked around the room before finding what he was looking for, cold locker #1212, and pulled the drawer out, revealing a woman I could barely recognize.

My mother's skin, aside from its faint grayish hue, looked like it had wrinkled beyond its natural age, deep folds in her bloated face appeared like the gills of a fat fish. Her once sandy locks had turned to rusted metal and had fallen off in chunks, leaving only wispy singular strands hanging on for dear life. If I didn't know better, I may have thought she was someone else entirely. A decade and a death will do that to a person.

"It's her," I said, unsure if Mr. Ostrowski was still even behind me, lost in the image of the bloated pile of gray death in front of me. "Is that all I have to do, just say it's her?"

"Well technically, yes." He sounded unsure of himself or like there was something else he wanted to say. "But I always like to give the families a few moments with the deceased. A sort of goodbye to their Earthly body, if you will."

"I don't think I need to ..." But the old man stuck out his hand, holding one finger up, scolding me.

"That's nonsense!" He put his hand on my shoulder in an act of reassuring authority. "That's your mother, after all. Have some respect."

Without saying anything else he vanished, leaving me alone in the cold metal chambers, surrounded by death. I could have left, refusing to listen to Mr. Ostrowski and his pathetic attempts at morally chastising me, but I stood there in my thoughts.

Who was he to cast judgment on me? He didn't know me or my mother. He didn't know the dysfunction that was my mother's overbearing presence over me. Or did he? A town of only locals, all descendants of one small village in Poland, who came here to build their lives and families all in one small community in Kolbe. Had I insulted him by my lack of urgency to say goodbye to my decaying mother?

As the memory of my mother's grasp on my life trickled into my thoughts, a cold clamminess grazed the back of my hand, like fingers intimately tickling their way up my knuckles until they wrapped around my wrist and grabbed it tight. My blood vessels bulged as whatever had a hold of me grabbed tighter, pulling me toward my mother's frozen body.

I looked down to see my mother's sewn-shut eyes were ripped open, dripping white masses staring straight at me. My mind took a moment to recognize it was her hands that grasped my wrist, pulling me closer toward her bulging body. I fought to rip her bony fingers from my hand, but her strength was supernatural, and I ended up on top of her bloated chest, jiggling like Jell-o and releasing a fowl smelling liquid from unknown orifices. My stomach gurgled, pushing sour bile up my throat until it settled in my mouth, burning my cheeks. Within an instant, green vomit began to pour over the edge of my mother's cold cabinet bed, retching from my gut and landing with a splash on the cold tile. The vomit pooled on the floor drain underneath the two of us, chunks sticking to the rim as the liquid filtered through. Tears streamed as I caught my breath but stopped when I felt the scratch of harsh kisses rubbing against my cheek.

"Get … away …" My throat burned from the acid that tore away at my flesh, and the words tumbled from my lips—barely audible. I scooched back on my hands, unable to force my weak body up from the floor, but I forgot my surroundings and ended up in a pile of my own puke. My stomach gurgled again, and I quickly wiped the mess on my jeans, ruining them. Flies began to swarm around the pile of sick, buzzing around the fragrant liquid—following it down the drain holes until they met their fate in the bottom of the sewer.

But my mother's reanimated body wouldn't take no for an answer. She jumped off of the cadaver bed to the floor, cracking and twisting as she crawled her way toward me—the fumes from her decaying body singeing the hairs in my nostrils the closer she got to me. My palms burned as I scooched backward, further away from my mother, friction from the cold tile meeting my skin and blistering them every inch I moved. Finally, I had backed myself into a corner with nowhere else to scooch away. I was frozen on the floor, still in disbelief.

Metal screeched as the sound of rollers running on tracks played behind me. One by one the clinking of steel corpse lockers opening filled the room like a symphony, all playing different notes of metal chimes in harmony. I whipped my body around and watched as each and every one of the bodies in their metal drawers crawled out of their lockers, creeping toward me as their disintegrating bones cracked and ripped out of their sockets.

Closer and closer the creaking corpses came, moaning something indistinguishable in unison. I tried to back away from the bodies, but with every step more and more cold lockers opened, and more and more former townsfolk of Kolbe came crawling to me, forced back to life by some sort of evil force. In seconds I was surrounded, unable to break free from the circle of reanimated death.

"Come to the dark, Franciska," the voices sang. As they inched closer to me, I could finally make out what they'd been repeating. "Come to the dark, Franciska. We're hungry, Franciska!"

When the bodies had crawled their way to my feet, my mother stood up from her cold coffin and sunk her angry stare into my watering eyes, forcing her presence down my throat until I was choking. In a flash she was on top of me, gripping my neck so tightly I thought my head would explode. Wretched brown fluids dripped from her body onto my face, filling the air with their putrid fumes of shit and death. But my throat was too constricted to puke again, so I sat there, inhaling the gasses that stung my eyeballs. I thrashed my body from side to side, attempting to loosen her grip, but her jagged fingernails pierced into my skin like sharp blades, igniting the smell of pennies as my own blood dripped down my body. Gripping on tighter, she used the strength of a thousand gods to whip me across the room, slamming my back into the open metal lockers.

"We're starving, Franciska," the bodies chanted again.

"Stop it, stop it, stop it!" My whole body ached as I screamed at the corpses over and over, crying to whoever would listen. I screamed until I couldn't anymore, until my body was weak and my voice hoarse and fading. I cried into my knees as I curled into a ball, frightened like a child having a nightmare. I stayed with my head in my lap until a knob jiggled and the door flew open, bright white light streaming into the dark mortuary chambers.

"Frankie?" A familiar voice spoke, like whispering petals on summer flowers. "Frankie, what's wrong?"

As if the world had ripped me apart and brought me back whole, Stella was in front of me, glowing from her glass skin, there to save me. No longer were the deceased former townsfolk haunting my subconscious, no longer was my mother back to life, suffocating me like she'd always done. All that stood in front of me in the cold metal morgue was the beautiful Stella, glowing like nothing could ever possibly be wrong.

"Come on," she said, gently grasping my wrist and helping me to stand. Her hold on me was like soft pressure pressing on all the right spots, nothing like my mother's rotten grip. Her voice was calming, never hoarse and demanding like my screams. "Let's get you out of here. I'll drive you home."

THE DEVIL'S FLESH

"**I** don't know why my uncle still leaves people alone in that place." Stella's black curls glowed auburn in the setting sun, the melting streetlights dancing on her profile as she drove me home in her small sedan. I felt an electric shock run down my back as she placed her hand on my thigh. "He knows most people aren't as comfortable with death as he is. I tell him all the time how he's creeping people out, but he never listens! And now, and now ..."

"It's okay," I whispered, "I'm fine."

I grabbed her hand and held it tightly in mine, assuring her that whatever had happened in the mortuary chambers was just a trick of my exhausted mind. I didn't tell her exactly what I had seen, mostly because I didn't want her to think I was crazy. But part of me worried that if I told her, I would drag her into it, ensuring her a life of dread at the hands of my own. She thought she was protecting me, but really, I was keeping her safe from things I didn't understand.

"I just ... can't lose you again," Stella said. She stopped at a red light and turned toward me, her eyes twinkling like the golden holiday lights outside. We kissed for the first time in ten years in her small car while we sat in front of Kolbe town square, the giant Christmas tree adorned in colorful sparkling ornaments.

The traffic light turned green, and we almost didn't notice, our moment of oneness shielding us from the reality beyond Stella's car doors. The only thing I could see were Stella's soft pink lips and the glittering snow falling behind her.

But Stella, sharp as she was, finally noticed we'd been sitting at the green light for far too long.

"Shit," I said, remembering my plans. "I was supposed to drive home tonight. But we just reunited, and I ..."

"You can't!" Stella jumped a little when her abrupt words flew from her mouth. It was as if I had startled her by mentioning my leaving. My heart ached knowing I had hurt her. "Didn't Uncle Ron tell you? The remains won't be ready for at least a week. And it's not just the remains, either. There's so much to do and to take care of, these things don't happen overnight! You just ... you can't leave yet, okay?"

I hadn't seen someone so upset at my leaving since I told my mother I was going to the city and never coming back. I had been thriving in the city, nailing a great job at the magazine, finding a close-knit group of friends that lived in the neighborhood, and even exploring the Queer scene out there—something I would have never had the chance to be a part of if I hadn't moved. But being close to Stella again made me think that maybe the slowness of small mountain life wasn't so bad after all. For the first time in a long time, I felt safe.

"Okay, okay," I reassured her by tickling her freckled neck, "I won't leave yet, I promise."

"Good." Her eyes settled on the road in front of her, which turned and twisted until we landed in the parking lot of the Kolbe Diner, whose white Christmas lights twinkled in the evening haze. The snow had just started to fall again, leaving flutters of frozen petals sprinkled onto the windshield. "Leaving during Sankta Lucia would be a crime against humanity. Plus, now we get to have our first dinner date."

The diner was much busier than the last time I had been there, almost every table or booth was filled with happy families or couples disguising their fights as intimate moments across small diner tables. The waitress called Jeannine greeted us at the front, her glasses now hanging from a fresh multicolored chain.

"My new friend!" Jeannine exclaimed as she waddled to us, menus in hand. She talked in circles as we followed her to the one empty table in the whole restaurant, a small corner booth in the back near the bathrooms. "So, have you decided to come to the Sankta Lucia Day celebration yet?"

"Ya' know Jeannine," I said while staring at Stella, "I think I just might."

"Oh, wonderful!" Jeannine gushed as her hands cradled her face. She looked at Stella and then back at me. "So how do you two know each other? Are you old friends?"

We both chuckled under our breath.

"Something like that," Stella said, winking at me.

Jeannine shuffled away from the table, leaving Stella and I to our first impromptu date in the smelly corner of the diner. Stella played with the plastic cups of coffee creamer, stacking them into towers and then flicking them down with her delicate finger. Her childlike innocence intrigued me, her beauty that of a full-grown woman but her charm that of someone who hadn't yet seen the jagged edges of life. Even though I knew that wasn't true.

"The Sankta Lucia Day celebration isn't even the best part," she said, still stacking and knocking over towers of creamers. "The real fun is the feast the night before."

"Feast?" I couldn't look away from her golden eyes; I was fixed to her glowing gaze of the destruction of buildings made of half-and-half. She could've said anything at that moment, all I cared about was being near her, being able to talk to her, stare into her. "What's that about?'

"You *have* to come, Frankie." Stella stopped playing Godzilla with her piles of mini coffee creamers and looked back into my eyes. I loved that she called me Frankie, the name I'd always preferred. Nobody else respected me enough. "The whole town gathers to eat a magnificent feast the night before Sankta Lucia. My uncle's going to host it this year. It's the best time, you can't miss it!"

The way she stared into me was like she could read all my thoughts and could manipulate them, too. Every time I felt a guttural pang of doubt it was wiped away with the thought of disappointing Stella again. It was as if my own thoughts had disappeared, and now the only thing I could think of was her. My head was swollen with pressure and confusion, I couldn't think for myself if I had tried. The prospect of true love, finally found, had taken over my brain and Stella was the only thing I saw. It wouldn't have mattered if I didn't want to go to the weird town feast, it was like I was *forced*.

"I will," I said, unable to control my own mouth. "It sounds fun."

"I knew you would." Stella's lips parted and raised to the same enchanting smile that made me fall for her back at the mortuary and back when we were teenagers. She kissed my trembling hand before getting up from the booth, leaving a glossed lip imprint on cracked skin. "I have to fix my makeup in the bathroom, don't leave me while I'm gone!"

"I wouldn't," and I meant it. I couldn't remember Stella having that strong of a hold on me in the past. I had left her, willingly, and although leaving was something I'd regret for an entire decade, it was still my choice. But now. It was like she could get me to do anything she wanted, just by smiling at me.

Nobody had ever had a hold on me like that before, at least not since my own mother. But the grips of Stella were nothing like the overbearing claws of the woman who raised me to be suspicious, untrusting of anyone besides her, all the while knowing she was the untrustworthy one. Stella I'd trust with my entire being.

My head fell sideways into my hand like a habit, watching through the tiny window as the snowflakes fell more quickly than before. My heartbeat rapidly to the rhythm of the snowfall; faster and faster it grew in my chest and on the wet ground outside. I didn't like the impending storms brewing as I sat in my janky booth at the top of a mountain, disconnected from anyone besides the inhabitants of this lonely town.

Storms weren't common in mountain towns like Kolbe. Here the snow just existed; it was born on the peaks of the Babias. It wasn't supposed to come tumbling down from the sky like war had broken out from the heavens—

The storms only come when evil is behind them.

The words rang in my ears, interrupting my daze and connecting me to something I'd forgotten, or pushed into the dark crevices of my mind. An image of an old priest with wrinkled gray skin singed behind my eyes, forcing me into a memory I couldn't get out of. The priest in my head grabbed a small child's hand with his decaying fingers and squeezed tightly as the child tried to wiggle free. He warned the child of the coming storms, repeating the words that rang even louder than before. My vision zoomed out and I could see that the child was me.

I shivered in my skin at the sight of this memory that I never knew existed. I tried to think back to my childhood in Kolbe, tried to create a clearer vision of it all, but the only thing I could remember was how desperately I had wanted to leave this place. And the further I tried to step back into my subconscious, the more clouded it became.

I attempted to push myself to think of the priest, think of my childhood, but the image just became distant and faded, until it was gone completely. The only clear image in my head was Stella. Beautiful Stella and her magnificent *everything*. My heart steadied as I pictured her walking back to the table, happy to see me.

But the only person walking toward me was an old decrepit man in worn clothing three sizes too big, limping and dragging his bandaged foot behind him. The diner had somehow emptied in a split second, leaving only me and the man remaining in the dining room. Even Jeannine had vanished, her excitable presence a noticed absence. When the man neared my booth, I thought he might pass right by me, remembering our unfortunate table right by the bathrooms.

But instead, the man slammed his disintegrating elbow onto my booth, falling into the bench, and struggling to gather his bones and body parts and sit in place safely. When he had found a comfortable enough position, he placed his palms on the table and stared into me with his red eyes.

"That woman smells of the devil's flesh." The old man wheezed and coughed like the words burned coming from his throat. He looked like he could die at any moment.

His accusations enraged me. I wanted to strangle the old fuck, but the thought of Stella being angry at me stopped me from doing what I wanted to. In my rage I hadn't noticed my fists were clenched, but I released them, putting them in my pockets just in case. The man stared at me still, white slobber leaking from the corner of his dry crusted lips.

"Hey, sir, I don't want any problems." My new plan was to have a conversation with the man, maybe help him in some way. He must have been confused, maybe he thought he was speaking to somebody he knew.

But my gentle demeanor shattered when his shaky hand knocked over a glass of water, spilling into my lap. His ribs cracked as he flopped forward over the table and stuck his face inches away from mine, snarling his rotted teeth. The dirty fingernail on his bony finger grazed my nose as he pointed in my face, breathing cold death into my nostrils.

"She's marked with the devil; she reeks of him!" Crawling closer and closer until he was completely on top of the table, he grabbed my shoulders and we shook together, his desperation leaking through his pores. "The Night of the Witches casts evil on this town! The darkness will prevail! Let the light shine! Let the light shine!"

I slid from his grip and out of the diner booth as quickly as I could, bending my neck to avoid getting touched again by the man's grotesque hands. But as I stood up from the booth, my hand foolishly grasped the table, giving the man a chance to wrap his bony fingers around my wrist, holding me in place

"Get off of me!" The man fell to the floor as I ripped his hands from my wrist, landing in a pile of bruises atop the dirty diner tiles. He moaned in pain, writhing at my feet.

I walked backward in slow motion, raising my hands in front of me like I'd committed a crime. I hadn't meant to hurt the old man; I just wanted him to leave me alone. But then his groans of pain and fits of wheezing turned to laughter, echoing through the empty diner walls and into the mountains around us. He cackled like a dying witch, globs of phlegm shooting from his throat as his wicked chuckle rang through the ceiling.

I ran through the sea of empty diner tables, half-drunken glasses of water and barely eaten burgers still sitting there waiting for their consumption. The diner stretched itself into a never-ending maze as I weaved through the remains of a once full restaurant. The man's laughter followed me through the miles of tile flooring and empty seats. I looked behind me as I ran forward, afraid that the man might have found some strength and speed, and it wasn't just his cackles that followed. I kept an eye on the man, watching his image fade into the distance, until my body slammed into something, and my head whipped to the front.

"Frankie, is everything okay?"

Stella had appeared from the snowy sky like an angel from above, and I was selfish enough not to notice until I had already slammed into her. Again, she had saved me from my delusions, gracing me with her comfort. But her presence only faintly drowned out the horrific man's laughter that still lingered in the air.

"Stella, where have you been?"

"I'm sorry, Frankie. I hope you're not upset. I just got to talking here with Jeannine, and we must have lost track of time!"

I blinked and the diner was full of patrons again, families of four eating a late meal, and couples making up after a fight. The old man behind me no longer cackled into the stormy sky, and no longer writhed on the floor in the distance. The diner was back to its normal size, back to business as usual with no indication that anything had gone wrong.

"It's fine," I said, confused and unamused at the mental trickery of the day. "Let's just eat our food and get the hell out of here."

The storm hurried outside the window next to our booth. Snow picking up faster in the raging wind, the windows clinked as little white pebbles flew into the glass. We ate mostly in silence, starved from the never-ending day. Every now and again we'd bring up some old story of our past together, reminiscing as we scarfed down pounds of beef slathered in ketchup and mustard. We didn't have to say much; it was as if no time had gone by.

Through the window, I caught a glimpse of something in the distance, watching me. If I closed my eyes for a moment, I could almost feel their breath on me, taunting me. I wiped the fogginess from the window with the sleeve of my flannel, hoping to get a better view.

Pressing my face to the edge of the glass, I saw the old man from before, standing in the parking lot, staring at me through the window. His eyes pierced through me, red lasers beaming their spotlights in my direction. He was saying something, mouthing it with obvious inflection. If I listened closely, I could almost make out what he was saying ...

"Don't go to the feast, Franciska." He sucked in the frozen air like it was his last breath. "The witches will eat you alive."

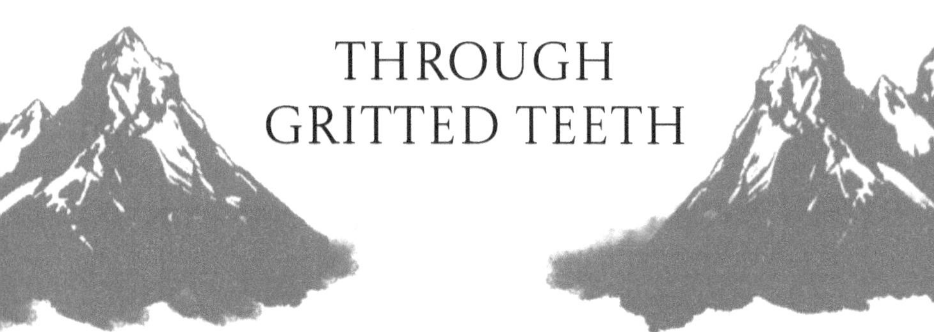

THROUGH GRITTED TEETH

"**Y**ou're telling me you didn't see that man?" I asked Stella, who was focused on the increasingly cloudy road. The drive away from the diner was glazed with fear, my neck aching from turning to see if the old man was still watching me from the parking lot.

"I'm sorry, Frankie," she said with the most soft-spoken little voice, like she pitied me. "I really don't know what you're talking about."

She looked ahead, eyes squinted through the cascading snowfall.

"Well, whoever he was, he told me not to go with you to the feast tomorrow night." I chuckled a little, making light of it but shaking inside of myself. "Said you smelled of the devil. But I think you smell like perfection …"

Stella's neck cracked as she whipped her head in my direction, her piercing golden eyes burning holes into my chest. She slammed her foot on the brake, jolting me forward, and sliding the car on the ice until it hit a small mound of piled up snow.

"I'm so sick of this …" Her teeth gritted, and her hands tightly bound the steering wheel, clenching the leather and metal until her knuckles turned bright red. Steam came from her mouth as the old sedan's heat started to fade away with the abrupt stop. "People in this town are always trying to ruin a good thing."

"Hey," I said softly, caressing her trembling arm, "he's just a crazy old man with nothin' to do, don't take it personally."

"I know." Her hands loosened their grip on the steering wheel, and her jaw unclenched, revealing once again the glowing smile I'd fallen in love with. "I just hate that everyone wants to change things here. They don't want to follow old traditions or remember their families long ago, the ones who come from our motherland, our only true home. Why do these people want to forget where they come from?"

Her eyes grew three sizes as the tears fell from her inflamed ducts, streaming down her perfect face. *Even when she cries she looks like an angel*, I thought, wanting to wipe her tears and tell her everything was okay but stuck staring in awe of the most magnificent creature I'd ever seen. She was like a child with a naive passion for saving the world, finding out that it was more complicated than recycling and treating everyone with kindness. Her heart was broken, thinking that the traditions she'd held close were at risk of falling apart. I wanted to save her from those thoughts, rip them to shreds, and protect her for life.

"They're idiots," I said, finally wiping her tears with my jacket sleeve and pulling her into my chest. "I would be honored to attend the feast as your date."

"Oh, Frankie!" Her face brightened as her tears dried to dust, vanishing into thin air. She wrapped her arms around my neck, squeezing tighter until she had climbed from the driver's seat onto my lap. She straddled me, kissing me softly on my ears and breathing her sweet breath into my pores. Her pelvis began to twist and roll, grinding into me until my underpants began to moisten. She inched her body downward, kissing my neck, then my breasts, then my stomach—until she'd reached my waist, traipsing along the line of my jeans and unbuttoning them.

Ripping each other's clothes off like teenagers out past curfew, we made love for the first time on the side of the mountain road, locking ourselves in and securing our bodies to each other for good.

Pulling the lever on the passenger seat, we flew backward, rolling over each other to switch positions until we'd both finished, respectively—our connected ecstasy mixing and spilling onto each other like we'd released our deepest demons. Stella crawled back over the middle console to the driver's seat and we both just stared at each other for a moment, unable to inhale deep breaths.

The stench of sweat and bodily fluids infiltrated the air in the small vehicle, our two flavors becoming one and overpowering our senses. But as I laid there unmoving, blissful as my heart steadied and my muscle aches relieved, Stella's face changed, telling another story. Her eyes no longer glowed golden rays but were dark—empty and unattracted. Her smile was hidden in her seriousness, a face I didn't recognize.

Stella grabbed the wheel without looking at me again. She shifted the sedan into reverse, backing away from the snow pile and turning the car around to continue our trip back to my mother's house. We drove ahead without speaking, and without touching. The picture of her loving softness that burned in my head was now stained, crumbling the colder her face became. Something told me I shouldn't ask.

POPPY PETALS

"I have some things to take care of," Stella said in the coldest, most blunt of terms. "I can't stay with you tonight, I'm sorry."

Her distance cut me deep into my chest, traveling zings of pain down to my stomach. Just minutes before we were making love, our bodies intertwined in the most magnificent of ways; two people becoming one. But her beaming energy no longer shined as bright, no longer reached out to touch me with its warmth. Her coldness just made me want her more.

"Please, Stella, don't make me beg."

"Franciska," her eyes pierced through me as her face finally turned to look at me, "I can't."

She hadn't ever called me by my *legal* name. I hated the sound of it.

Reaching over me to open my door, as if I couldn't do it myself or like I was some immature child who couldn't take no for an answer, she made herself clear. My stomach sunk to the floor as she sped away, gravel and puffs of powdery snow trailing behind her. My aching heart broke when she didn't even look behind her, acknowledging that she still cared for me. She was gone; I was alone.

The front yard of my mother's house was a mess from the wind and piling snow, dead petals from flowerpots knocked over and shards of broken clay pottery strewn about the lawn. The porch sank deeper as the flakes piled on top of it, crushing the rotting wood with their weight. The stairs creaked with each step, and the railing wobbled. Gusts of wind forced the front door open as soon as I turned the lock, my fingers still attached to the keys. I was in—safe and warm—but my mother's house felt dark; empty. Nothing could make me forget about Stella and her abrupt departure. I wanted her close to me again; I craved her scent. But a warm bath and a good night's sleep would have to do.

Zula and the absence of her jingling bell collar stopped me before heading upstairs to the bath, remembering the poor old cat with her missing tufts of fur and broken teeth. She hadn't eaten since the morning and was probably starving half to death in her skinny fragile body. I reluctantly stumbled through the dark to the kitchen, shaking the dry food in a bag from the cabinet. But still no jingle jangled nor did aching paws pounce on the wood floors.

"Zula," I called. "Here kitty, kitty."

But nothing came forward. The wind screaming through the broken window reminded me that she'd climbed out of there before and must have been finding herself dinner out in the wild. I pitied her, wondered if she'd even make it back.

The staircase winded and turned, my clumsy feet tripping on each unlit step. Feeling for stability in the dark, I put my hands on the steps above me and crawled the rest of the way up, until I'd reached the landing and could find my way standing to my mother's bedroom.

Poppy petals for sleep and unease.

My mother's teachings hadn't left me yet. The jar of mostly dried flower petals stood on the counter where I'd picked it up from the floor and left it, enticing me to pour the homemade potpourri into the steaming bath I'd made. It called to me, the sweet scent whispering about forgetting my troubles. I poured it in, turning the bath into a garbage pit of blood-red flaking petals, but the smell that exuded from the cloudy water calmed my heavy chest, and I got in.

The water stung my frosted toes, but I pushed in anyway, nearly falling into the overdrawn clawfoot bathtub. The poppy potpourri floated around me in swirling waves, getting caught in the crooks of my cooking body. Steam rose from my thighs and traveled up to the ceiling, creating a mist of floral air.

I sunk under the clouds, soaking in the simmering concoction that I'd made to soothe my bones. My eyes closed under the heated blanket of water, and I stayed there a moment, blowing bubbles through my nose. When I arose from the depths of the tub the steam seeped into my pores, numbing my joints and easing the weight from my body. Leaning my head against the cool porcelain I drifted away, my empty body floating in the sizzling bathtub and my eyes rolling back into my head, following the dark paths of slumber.

The sky was black except for the daggers of white snow that pummeled down on top of me. I couldn't see for any long distance in front or around my body, the storm came down so quickly, a stark bright contrast to the deep dark night. The cold wind swirled around me, sealing me in place—unable to move my limbs. The world had opened up millions of lightyears into the depths of space, but I was frozen in the empty void.

Whistling gusts blew from behind me and carried me through the blizzard, warping the sky around me into a dizzy black and white and gray mess. Landing on the tip of a mountain, a single flame flickered in the distance, dancing with the waves of the wind until it faded into the night, burning out with the gusts. The entire sky blackened; the deepest dark shadowed the whole planet into nothingness.

Laughter erupted in the directionless void, soon followed by more and more voices, emptiness interrupted by the increasingly louder cackling coming from the peaks of the unseeable mountains. Moving even an inch to try and run from the horrific screeching laughter could mean falling to my death, so I stayed grounded, covering my ears to shield them from the aching sounds of whoever, or whatever, was living in the mountaintops.

My eyes squeezed tightly together, hoping to rid myself of the nothingness; hoping to wake up and be back to earth, back in the tub full of calming powdery warmness.

"Will yourself awake, Franciska."

"Will yourself awake."

My bones trembled in the cold black hole, stuck in the darkness with the sinister laughing and nothing else to protect me in empty space. The voices still filled the freezing air, but if I listened closely, they began to change. The cackling transformed into something more uniform, something more melodic, like they were chanting, singing.

"The lights of Lucia burn out tonight ..."

The chant repeated until it was louder than ever, like the voices shouted above me, around me—from within me. The wind was like sharp knives, piercing through my ear drums, reminding me that I was stuck out there in the void, alone and without my own screams to save me.

The thoughts in my head were the only communication I could muster, so I listened. I listened deeply, and intently.

"Awake, Franciska."

"Awake ..."

Repeating the words to myself was my only comfort, like there was hope to leave the snowy purgatory I was doomed to stay in. If my concentration slipped, who knows what other darkness could have come lurking behind the corners of the mountains. I breathed in and held in, willing myself to leave this state.

"Leave this place, Franciska."

"It's not too late."

The wind and impending snowfall punched me in my gut, forcing the breath I was holding out of my mouth in a gasp. Weakened, I fell backward into the snow and rocky peaks. My fingers grazed my swollen belly, finding their way through globs of warm wetness, slimy exposed organs and miles and miles of intestines. My hands slipped through the heaps of bloody meat, stroking the tissue that squished in the crooks of my fingers. Feeling my way around the warm bloody mess, soft fur tickled my wrists; bristles connecting with the hairs that stood straight from my arms. Was it an animal?

"It's time to wake up, Franciska ..."

Transporting back to earth and reality, the tub still held me in place, head against the porcelain and an aching in my neck. The once steaming water sloshed against my stomach and splashed lukewarm droplets into my face. A single drop traveled down my nose and melted into my mouth. The taste of rotting meat absorbed into my tongue, releasing me from my grogginess. My eyes ripped open, glued-on crust breaking apart as the lids painfully separated. My stomach rumbled glancing into the murky poppy water.

In my lap laid the carcass of an opossum, eyes bulging from their sockets and mouth wide open, tongue sticking out. Its flesh was ripped open from the neck to the belly, drenched in blood and exposed intestines. My fingers were weaved into the thing's organs, like I had been playing with them—

I pushed the rotting animal off my lap and into the water, jumping up quickly but slipping on the porcelain and falling onto the tile floor outside of the tub. Tumbling over into a fetal position, my stomach wretched and dark brown vomit propelled from the depths of my gut, spraying onto the walls, dripping down to the baseboards. Little slurps and smacking sounds rang in my ear, accompanied by scratches of claws on tile.

My aching eyes turned slowly to my peripheral, revealing a dark blob of something encroaching on my personal space, inches away from my face. My head perked up and my eyes focused, the blurry figure becoming clearer with every breath I took. Zula was back, enjoying a nice warm meal made of my vomit. Her green marble eyes locked with mine, staring at me as she licked up the remnants of my disgust. A low grumble came from her throat as the disheveled cat finished up the last of her supper.

"Zula," I roared at her, "stop it!"

The hungry cat hissed at my attempts at discipline, showing her teeth and the entirety of her mangled mouth. Her chest puffed as she straightened her back and walked one paw in front of the either: slowly approaching her newfound enemy in me.

My hands pressed firmly on the floor, inching my butt backward in slow motion. I scooched my body with my heels until my back slammed into the cold porcelain of the bloody tub behind me, trapping me in the small bathroom with no way out. Zula picked up her pace, claws clopping on the tile in a prance. Prepared for an attack, I shielded my face and neck with my arms, breathing in the flesh and guts that lingered on my skin.

But Zula walked past me, grumbling a low growl that permeated from her small frame. Through the crack in the fold of my arm, I watched as the old cat stood on her back paws and reached over the edge of the tub, retrieving her bloody opossum treat and dragging him to the other side of the bathroom. She stared at me with red eyes, growling from the pit of her stomach, chowing away at her first-place prize for a good night's hunt.

"Enjoy your dinner," I said, gagging. I picked myself from the floor, gently and quietly so as to not disturb Zula and the grotesque scene in front of me. Tip-toeing out the door, I shut it behind me, locking her in there with the mess. I'd pick up the bones and other remnants the next day. Zula could shit and piss on the floor all night for all I cared.

Grabbing a rag from my mother's dresser and wiping off the rest of the opossum guts from my arms, a little pink radio fell at my feet, hitting the wood floor right on the corner that held the *on* button. Static screamed for a moment until the signal caught on and crackled voices began to speak through the speaker. Throwing the rag onto the floor, I laid my unclothed body in my mother's satin sheets, allowing whatever came on the radio to play freely. By the sounds of it, the dial was already set to the weather station. Like the snow and wind from outside the shaking window frame were in the booth with the weather reporter, his voice came through in labored gusts.

"The massive snowstorm that has meteorologists scratching their heads was not anticipated nor can it be predicted. We have tried to follow the pattern of the cyclone, but it seems to be traveling in an unusual manner that we've never seen with past storms of this size. Due to the nature of the blizzard and the strange manner in which we are seeing it accumulate, we are encouraging everyone within ten miles of Kolbe County to take shelter at home until the snow passes and the roads are clear."

WARM BELLIES

December 12th

Bright winter sun shone through the windows, exposing the world to my uncovered body, curled into a ball within the folds of my mother's rose gold satin sheets. Spreading out like a starfish, I laid there a while, brushing my fingers on the smooth silky bedding that glistened with the snowy sun shining through the frosted glass. The smoothness of the satin on my palms made them light, like they were floating in the clouds, until my hand reached too far up by the pillows and touched something coarse, scratchy, matted. Zula was asleep on the pillow, snoring through the bloody crust on her nose.

My gag reflex erupted remembering the treat Zula brought to my lap, imagining her piercing through the skin and fur, ripping the thing open, and devouring the rotting meat clean from the bone. What a mess the bathroom must have been, slathered in blood and guts and brown puke. But the bathroom—*didn't I lock her in there?*

The phone rang, muffled by the pile of clothes on top of it that broke my suspicions about Zula. The long twisted phone cord had winded itself around a pair of my mother's lacy white underwear, gripping to the plastic twirls even as I plucked it off with pinched fingers and turned-away eyes. The receiver stuck to my hand as I grasped it, holding it as close to my ear as possible without touching it to my face and transferring whatever stickiness lay in the holes of the earpiece.

"Hello?" I said, still trying to hold back the puke forming in my throat while shooing Zula out of the bedroom. She hopped from the bed to the squeaky wood floor, bones creaking with the turning of her neck to hiss at me before trotting away down the stairs.

"Franciska, just who I was looking for!" The old man's Slavic voice was crisp as day, even with the harsh wind blowing through the receiver. He must have been standing outside while talking to me. I pictured him on the front porch, staring into the cloudy skies, long but untangled phone cord trailing behind him from inside the morgue. "Is that your vehicle parked out in our lot? I think you'd better get back to it before it becomes one with the heaps of ice out here. Weatherman says the storm's coming back tonight two-fold."

I sighed, annoyed that he refused to call me *Frankie*, and that I had to go back there again so early. But I couldn't forget the reason I was there. I was paying my respects and getting paid to do it. I couldn't back out now.

"Any more word on the estate?"

"Oh," he groaned, "we can discuss all that when you're here. You better hurry, now, don't want to get stuck in the blizzard, that wouldn't be very good at all."

That vouldn't be very gud. Mr. Ostrowski's accent tickled my memory, and I fought the urge to chuckle; the way he pronounced the words reminded me a little of my grandmother, maybe even a little of my mother.

The receiver clicked on the other end before I could say goodbye, the mortician needing the last word, assuming I'd agreed to meet him without even asking. But he was right, I did need my truck. But did I have to walk to the morgue, like I was a child again exploring the confines of the tiny mountain town? Stella was the whole reason I was even left without my Bronco, but where was she now?

I called the number Stella had given me for her apartment line. No answer.

I waited ten minutes and called again. Still no answer.

I grasped the pillowcase in my anxiety, finding a small lump in the center. Pulling it out, the pouch of oregano appeared, soothing my nerves. I didn't remember grabbing it from the pocket of my jeans before going to bed, but the night, as chaotic as it was, was sure to inhibit bits of my memory.

The sky cried in wispy flurries outside the window, the wind blowing them sideways, making room for the storm that wouldn't stop coming back to our little hole in the mountains. My worries about Stella would have to follow me all the way through the increasingly abundant snow and to her uncle's office, shutting off until I figured out what was going on with the supposed sum of money I still hadn't received, the mystery of my mother and her secret stash still unsolved.

I rushed through heaps of snow and rumbling skies to the morgue, a luxury of the small town being that it was less than a mile away from my mother's place. Christmas lights on streetlamps and lining the roofs of houses brightened the gloomy air; candles burning in the windows of people's homes welcomed the soon approaching Sankta Lucia holiday. It felt like a familiar home again for a moment, like my mother had never left, hadn't chased me out of there. A smile greeted my lips as I parted the dusty white road with my footsteps. I arrived at the morgue in less than ten minutes.

Mr. Ostrowski waited for me on the icy front stoop, smoking a cigar and staring into the dark clouds, exactly as I'd imagined when the wind whistled through the phone lines. When his wandering mind caught sight of me walking up the stone drive, his eyes lit up. He smiled with mangled teeth, waving hurriedly with long sharp fingernails and wrinkled loose skin. He snuffed out his stogie on the railing, ashes and sparks flying away with the harsh wind and leaving a black burn mark on the wooden rail.

"Miss Bosko!" He greeted me with inviting arms, like my arrival was a joyous occasion. "Please come in."

"I'm really just here to get my car." My heart skipped at the thought of offending the old man who clearly just wanted company, but without any progression into the contents of my mother's estate—*without a damn check*—there wasn't any real reason for me to be there.

"Your vehicle will still be in the lot when we're done," he said, spittle spraying from the corners of his lips. "I might even offer you the news regarding your mother's accounts. Please, come in before the storm shows up again and knocks you on your *dupa*."

I followed him to his tiny taxidermized office, dark shadows casting over the dead animals displayed about the room. The warm glow from his green desk lamp soothed my frozen fingertips, filling the walls with its yellow light. Mr. Ostrowski sat in his leather office chair and shuffled through piles of papers in disarray before finding the packet he'd needed. Adjusting his glasses down the bridge of his nose, he motioned with his hand for me to sit in the smaller visitor's chair on the other side of the desk. I sat, patiently for a moment, but my stomach sank to the floor and sweat formed on my hands; my heart pumped in irregular patterns in and out of my chest.

"Where's Stella?" My palms habitually wiped themselves on the knees of my black jeans, my legs shaking along with my fingers, nervous and broken hearted like I'd lost her to something tragic. Mr. Ostrowski looked up at me, fixing his glasses back into their proper position. "I'm sorry, I just haven't heard from her and I'm a little worried. Is she not working today?"

Bloodshot eyes stared through me. His bushy eyebrows scrunched together, and his mouth tightened into a wrinkly ball. He put the stack of papers back onto the desk, pushing them to the side to stare even more intently into my soul. My heartbeat even more rapidly.

"I see you've become very close with my niece," he said, a low grumble coming from the pits of his gut. "Very quickly, at that."

"We knew each other a long time ago," my voice wavered. "We've sort of ... reunited. I don't mean to pry into her life or anything. I just care about her, that's all."

The mortician stared into me for another moment, until his face cracked into erupting laughter, brightening like a ripe strawberry. Slapping the wood desk with his tremored hands, I noticed the stacks of gold rings on his chubby wrinkled fingers, clinking against the wood as he tried to catch his breath. Lifting his hands from the desk to wipe the tears that had formed under his eyes, he looked at me again, this time with a softer face.

"I'm fooling you, *Franciska*. Don't think I'm such an old man that I don't know about you kids and your *modern romance.* I may not understand it, nor will I ever. But I sure as hell know what a couple in love looks like!" Remnants of laughter sat on his tongue, and I imagined them forming at the belly and tightening in his broad chest. He struggled to hold it inside. "She's helping to prepare for The Feast this evening. No need to worry yourself with her whereabouts—she's just doing what she loves. *Sankta Lucia* is very important to her, to all of us. You came at a very special time, young lady."

"Some say." My mind drifted to my mother dancing in the kitchen, long sandy hair tied back with a peacock green ribbon that flowed in the air with each movement. Her belled sleeves whipped around her, twisting around her waist, and getting caught in the loops in her jeans. She smiled as her hips swayed, and it was like everything was okay, as if the fear I held in me for my mother hadn't existed, like I wasn't constantly worried which version of her I'd get. As I grew older, I tried to distance myself, but there were still moments I'd catch her dancing in the kitchen, cigarette in hand and a silk scarf tied into her hair. I never wanted much from my mother, not even affection, mostly because it wasn't consistently offered. But when I grew away from her, I stopped wanting anything at all, not even a phone call, until I learned of her death and the money she'd left me. *Oh my god, the money*. I slipped back into the present quicker than I'd left. "So, you said you had an update on the estate?"

"Oh, yes!" Mr. Ostrowski scooted the packet of papers back in front of his sight, fixing his glasses back to their proper position all the way at the end of his nose bridge. "The estate lawyers have been delayed in getting up here due to the storms. But if all goes well tonight, we should be hearing from them tomorrow."

"If all goes well?" Mr. Ostrowski's eyes turned downward when I asked, suspicious or perhaps embarrassed of something unknown. "What do you mean?"

"Oh, Franciska" His eyes looked down and the gears turned in his head. His lips tightened again but into a thin sliver of nothing. He licked his lips, grabbing the bottle of blackberry brandy that sat on the corner of his desk, pouring it into two glasses that appeared from nowhere. "You're overthinking things. Grief can do that to a man, make 'em think a little too much, and for a little too long, if you ask me. But you know what I've learned in all my years on this *gówno*—this *shit*—planet? All a man really needs is a drink. Or *woman*, in your case."

Mr. Ostrowski slid the second glass over to my hand, gripping the clear container like it was meant to fit exactly. My fingers wrapped around the foggy drink, instinctually clanking it against the glass in the mortician's hand, toasting to the strangest part of my life to date—or maybe just to nothing.

We drank together for over an hour, reminiscing about the parts of Kolbe I had forgotten, the parts of my mother I'd never known. He told me stories of Lucy when she was younger, gushing how she was the most beautiful girl he'd ever seen. I was dazed in drunkenness as he went on and on about her strong convictions, cementing it into me that *Lucja* was a natural born leader. I thought of the way she treated me as a child, affection built on how much I had impressed her that day, how little I had gotten in her way. I suppose that natural born leaders can become tyrants, too, if they try hard enough. We kept drinking until the mortician had poured the last drops of the bottle into our glasses, our stomachs warm with the rich brandy.

The last dribbles of brown alcohol graced my lips, and I slobbered them up, savoring their sweetness as they traveled across my tongue and down to my sizzling belly. With liquid courage and a new bond between the two of us, I felt comfortable with Mr. Ostrowski. Possibly the most comfortable I'd felt my entire trip, even counting the time I'd cherished with Stella.

Mr. Ostrowski finished his drink and slowly rose from his leather chair, gripping on to the arm rests to keep balanced. I took his lead, standing up from my guest seat, leaning on the desk to avoid stumbling over like a log. The brandy had done its job. The old man grabbed the two empty glasses, hitting them together as he held both with two pinched fingers. His head tilted a little toward the door, indicating without words that it was time for me to leave.

He led me through the dark hallway and to the front door, a clear demand that I was no longer welcome, but he still did it with red cheeks and a jolly demeanor. He patted me on the back, like an old friend who'd come for a short visit and had stayed a little too long, but he wanted to be polite. Maybe he was just buttering me up so I wouldn't complain about how long my mother's estate was taking to handle. But I couldn't let him leave without igniting my curiosity. I felt a closeness with him that I hadn't felt in a long time, and I knew that if anyone could help me, it'd be him.

"Hope to see you tonight at the feast!" He patted me one more time on the back, an awkward but assured friendship, now fully formed.

"Mr. Ostrowski," I said, turning around to face the man before walking away. "Do you know anything about this thing called The Night of the Witches?"

The flushed red color of his cheeks vanished, stripped away into pale emptiness. His eyes bulged from their sockets, enhancing the veins and blood vessels that crawled around the yellowed sclera. His hand tremored and his grip loosened, dropping the fragile cocktail cups on the ground. The glass shattered into a million pieces, creating a crystal rainbow of speckled light across the dark morgue walls.

"Oh, these stupid hands," he grumbled, grabbing his handkerchief and bending over to pick up the shards one by one. "Old men can't be trusted with anything, now, can they?"

"Here, let me help you," I said, nearly bumping heads with the old man as I bent down to help pick up the glass. But when I had just barely grazed the sparkling shards, wrinkled fingers waved in my face, swatting my hand away.

"No need to help," he said, his voice shaking like his hands. "We've been sitting here chatting for much longer than we needed to be. It's getting late and there's much to do today! Better get to your truck before the storms come in harder, don't wanna get stuck out here."

I offered to help once more but was waved off and nearly shoved out of the door. I didn't want to burden the old man any longer, but I couldn't help but recognize that my silly questions had more effect on him than I'd anticipated. I worried I'd upset him, ruining any chances at the bond I thought we'd cultivated. I was worried that my questions were so intrusive, he wouldn't want to speak to me ever again. But before I reached the bottom step of the front porch, the sound of shuffling feet behind me became louder as they approached my shoulder.

"Franciska," the old man's voice whispered. "Don't go poking around in silly things like that. Just pay it no mind, you hear me?"

THE MOUNTAINS
REMEMBER

The Bronco was covered in packed snow, but in my drunkenness, I sloshed a giant pile onto the ground in a second, not even worrying about the clarity of the windshield itself. Contemplating walking back so I didn't risk driving inebriated, I threw my hand at the idea and got in the truck anyway. I knew I shouldn't have been driving in that condition, especially with the blizzard coming in harder, but I couldn't stay there any longer, either.

The engine roared without trouble, even though every dial or gear or button in the interior cab was frozen. I popped *Trompe le Monde* back into the tape player, starting my road trip song-list over again. The volume was turned down low, a smart decision made by my past self. I cranked the dial up as high as it would go and pressed *next* on the car stereo until I'd found the song I was looking for. "Bird Dream of the Olympus Mons" blasted from the speakers, drowning out my thoughts. The tape skipped a few times as the Bronco bumped along the old sleet-slicked roads.

The road to nowhere led me through the outskirts of town, an unplanned trip caused by tipsiness and a need to calm my mind before the impending feast. If Stella would be busy all day setting up for tomorrow's celebration, and there wasn't anything to take care of regarding my mother or her estate, I thought it might make for an interesting day to explore the place I'd tried to forget.

The cracked old road led me to the main road in Kolbe, which led me to town square, where all the town's amenities were housed. The main road was much less riddled with potholes and sunken in bits, and the music played smoothly from the car speakers.

"Into the mountains ...

I ... will ... fall...

Into the mountains ..."

The town was empty save for the candles burning in every shop window, townsfolk excited to usher in the Sankta Lucia holiday with cheer, a sentiment I'd never related to. The whole population must have been up the mountain, huddled in the ancient church where all celebrations were held. Their cheeks flushed with church wine and true happiness; smiles on their faces as they glided along the banisters with miles of garland traipsing behind, lighting candles with long brass igniters and dancing in the smoke from the cheap white wax.

The lonely road took me to the front entrance of the Kolbe Library, my Bronco parking itself in the closest spot to the door, a speck in the sea that was the emptiest parking lot I'd ever seen. Although no cars were in the lot, there were also no chains on the doors, no "closed" sign in the window, and the lights were turned on. In a small town like Kolbe, it was perfectly possible for the librarian to have walked to work that day, even with the approaching storms. The door was cracked open a little, inviting me in.

I whispered a *hello* as I took my first steps in the blue carpeted library, expecting the librarian to greet me. But nobody was behind the desk, and no readers sat in chairs or wandered in the aisles of books. I couldn't possibly have been in there alone, but as I stood in the quietest ever house of books, it seemed alone I truly was.

"Into the mountains ...

I ... will ... crawl..."

I hadn't planned on coming to the library, so there wasn't any book in particular that I felt called to. Neither did I have a section of the seating area picked out, a cup of black tea in my hand begging to be sat upon the nearest end table as I melted away in a soft upholstered chair, lost in some fictional story land.

My feet stopped walking in endless circles when I'd found myself in the Historical Nonfiction section, surrounded by old decrepit books written by historians long passed. A faded green monster of a book titled *The History of Kolbe* jumped off from the shelves, landing face-up at my feet. Curious, I picked it up, holding it tightly in my hands like I'd found the secret to life. The empty space on the bookshelf was accompanied by rows of Kolbe birth and death records, dating back to the 1600's. I grabbed as many as I could stack in my arms, bringing them back to a small white table that seemed to simply appear in the middle of the Nonfiction section.

The green history book cracked open like it hadn't been read in decades, dust particles flying up into the stuffy air. Flipping through the pages was like studying for an exam I had no intention of ever passing; I was finding nothing of use, even with no intention of finding anything at all.

My mother trickled into my thoughts, dancing around my mind with her flowing dress and silk scarf tied around her hair, tip toeing like a ballerina to the top of a misty mountain that appeared in the distance. She practically floated, her ethereal body disintegrating into smoke masking the mountains that loomed over everything, creating a shadow of darkness in my head. The smoke traveled down the covered mountain until it was swallowing me whole, shielding me from the light that peaked through the cracks.

It swirled around me until it dissipated at my feet, clearing the skies and focusing my eyes to my mother at the top of the rock, still dancing, her long sleeves wisping around her and wrapping themselves around her waist. She rocked and swayed haphazardly in the wind, twirling and twirling until her foot slipped and her leg gave out, sending her flying hundreds of feet down to the frozen ground. As she descended down the snow and rocks, I caught a glimpse of her face—scarred and skin shredded, with a mangled jaw hanging from its hinges. Sharp teeth stuck out from her lips in abundance, far too many of them to resemble that of a human mouth.

Without knowing, my fingers flipped through the pages of the Kolbe history book, dust suspended in the air, and my mind still lost in my day-dreams. But with nothing but smoke and the burned image of my mother's wretched face in my head, my eyes crossed for a moment before settling back to the fluorescent lights of the library. My thumb stopped flipping, landing on a textured page—bumpy letters and indented line drawings, like it was written by hand with ink and quill. The corners were singed, black, like an attempt at burning the whole book had been made but ultimately failed. The raised old-timey lettering on the page was starting to fade but still read clearly: *Beware the Night of the Witches.*

Everything in the library froze in time and my eyes focused on the words in front of me; the answer I'd been searching for days had finally revealed itself. Only a page and a half were dedicated to the mystery of the mythical event, a mere mention of the words that stuck to me since I'd heard the old man scream them at me. Too many times had I allowed this town to make me think I was crazy; it was time to start figuring out what the *hell* was going on in Kolbe.

"In Polish Folklore, The Night of the Witches signifies the opening of the portal between Hell and Earth, allowing spirits of all kinds to enter. According to the story, the Witches came from the Babia Góra—Mountain of the Crones—in Krakow, where they would cast spells and enact rituals in order to serve their leader.

On the night of December 12th, one night before the Scandinavian tra-dition of Sankta Lucia, and one of the darkest nights of the year, it is said that the Witches of Babia Góra meet to cast their spells, and offer sacrifices, including children, to the world down below. They feed on their prey, using the victim's bodies as fuel for their mystical powers of evil.

Whenever the Witches meet with their coven in the mountains, hazardous snowstorms start brewing, often trapping the innocent townsfolk in their homes for fear of being lost or killed in the piles and piles of ice and snow.

But their rituals are not without fail, for if the sun rises, interrupting their dances and chants, the spell will be broken, damning the witches to an eternity in hell, without their powers of evil to release them.

In Kolbe myth and legend, it is said that the Polish migrants that founded the town may be true descendants of the Crones of Babia Góra. The Babia mountains that surround Kolbe are even named after the Babia Góra, after all.

If Sankta Lucia celebrates the courageous Saint Lucia, who brings with her the light of the heavens, then The Night of the Witches is the exact opposite. According to folklore, the Night of the Witches is about feeding the darkness—the underworld of evil. And if the tales are true, then it seems the two celebrations are in direct contrast—one celebrates the good, and the light. And the other celebrates the dark.

The tales of those before us will forever haunt us in their obscurity but leaving them from the records would mean to erase a part of this town's inception, possibly doing more harm than good.

The history of Kolbe cannot be taught completely if not for the mention of this fateful night nor those dark misty mountains in Poland. Our history, our culture, is more embedded and intertwined with these tales than one can teach in history books and town records.

Kolbe is bred from the soil of Babia Góra."

I shut the old book, the last of the collected dust poofing out into the unfiltered library air, circling around a small lamp sitting on the corner of the table. Sweat trickled down my neck, a symptom of my racing heart and the beating fluorescents above my unkempt head. Why were the people of this town so uneasy about this old myth; they couldn't possibly think it was real, could they?

I scoffed at the thought, a judgmental grunt echoing into the empty building and fighting with the shrieking wind outside. The towns peoples' simple-mindedness as to believe such a silly myth was disheartening; it made me pity them. But the storms raging more intensely outside, and the fluttering that creeped its way into my chest, was enough to spook the part of me that couldn't reconcile with superstition.

The stacks of birth and death records glared at me, tempting my curiosity with their worn corners and beveled paper edges. I started with the oldest set I could find—dating back to 1701. The people who built Kolbe spoke loudly through the pages, their stories told between the lines of text, some of them having only lived a few years on Earth, others meeting their tragic fates of disease or disaster. Their spirits hovered above me, enveloping me in the energy of those who came before me; the energy of the folks who made this town from nothing, having come from the mountains in Poland to try and establish themselves in a new world and just looking for a little piece of home. Reading their names made them real, helping me find an appreciation for Kolbe for what it was and not what it had done to me.

Admiring the stories told through dates and locations, I came upon a page that was more tattered than the others. Similarly to the page on Night of the Witches in the history book, this particular sheet was indented with fancy lettering and smeared, like it had been written by hand. A list was written in small letters across the entire page, containing at least a hundred names if not more. At the top of the list was a name I'd recognize anywhere, the coincidence masking itself as a sign from the universe:

Stanisława "Stella" Ostrowski
Birth date: *October 24, 1798*
Death date: *Unlisted*

Stella ached in my bones; the memory of our last encounter burned into me like stabbing knives. I hadn't thought of her in hours, something that seemed impossible before leaving the house and drinking my weight in brandy. Now her supple pink lips floated across my mind again; her tall and voluptuous body sinking into me further, and further—

It must have just been an old relative of hers, long passed but gifting her name to the most beautiful creature on the planet. But with a quick glance another name caught my eye, sparkling in the fluorescents like a message from the gods.

Lucja "Lucy" Bosko
Birth date: *August 17, 1707*
Death date: *Unlisted*

The coincidence was starting to feel more like a warning. My mother hadn't been named after anyone; she was the first *Lucja* in the family. I remembered my grandmother telling me that when I was a child, long before she lost her memories and even longer before she passed away. On her lap sitting on a recliner in her floral living room, she told me the story of my mother's name, how it was a name she'd loved since she was a girl, after learning about the Swedish holiday of *Sankta Lucia*. It was her that brought the tradition back to Kolbe, my grandmother who instilled the meaning of the festival of lights into this town and kept it alive long after her death. My grandmother was the reason for the most cherished event in town, something I'd forgotten in my absence. It had to be a coincidence. My mother couldn't possibly be the same Lucja from the book, that would be ludicrous, bonkers—*insane.*

But her birthday was also August 17th ...

No. The thought was ridiculous. My mother was young and vibrant growing up, not an old crone who one day just vanished from the face of the earth. I was only gone ten years, not a lifetime. *I saw her fucking dead body.* I saw it with my own eyes and even in my delusions. I saw it when it was cold, lifeless and gray, and I saw it again when she reanimated into whatever being it was that tried to eat me in the morgue. I even saw her in my dreams and all over the town in her poppy flowers, her ideas, her influence. I couldn't get away from my mother if

I tried, even when I left this town thinking I'd never look back. I was a fool to think I could rid myself of her.

I scoured the list of remaining names, looking for something to connect the madness together or something to make *me* seem a little less mad. The smeared names were difficult to read but had one very important detail in common: their births all occurred hundreds of years before I sat reading them from a book at the Kolbe Library, and not one of them had a death date listed. Ten, fifty, hundreds of names I sifted through, and their fates all ended the same—*Unlisted*.

It didn't make sense, for all those Polish immigrants, all those founders of this town, to have just simply disappeared, every single one on the page but with no explanation for why. Each person on the list had lived but never died, the end of their existence wiped from history, forever buried in a hidden cave in the mountains, protected in eternity by the rock and snow.

The ink bled from the page and onto my finger as I looked for someone on the list, anyone, with their death-date recorded. I didn't know what finding those dates would do or what it meant, but the coincidence that felt like a warning was now starting to nestle in my eardrums like a tornado siren, alerting me to urgency. And at the bottom of the list, I found the reason for the alarm. If one familiar name on the list was just by chance, and two was a coincidence, then what did three make?

The final name was a Mr. Roland Ostrowski, born in 1751 and died—unsurprisingly, never. Yet another familiar person on the unusual list of people who should have been long gone; it couldn't just be happenstance. Something was wrong with this town, with the people that founded it, and possibly those who still inhabit it, too. Was the Night of the Witches a ploy somehow? Some secret meeting of dark souls, gathered together to prey upon those who don't wish to follow the evil traditions of their past? What was the fucking point?

"*She wants to slurp your innards like soup.*"

"Who said that?" I whipped my head to scan the room, still nobody was there.

"The blood is extra tasty when your dead mommy made it." Screaming into my ear, the invisible speaker sounded like they were right next to my face, centimeters away.

High pitched laughter screeched from all directions, chaos of increasing sound and flickering lights. The names in the book melted off the page, bleeding into a pool on the white table, and dripping into my lap. The laughing went on, getting louder and more abrupt— maniacal.

I shut the bloody book, tossing it to the side where it tumbled to the carpeted floor with the rest of the stack. I didn't worry about pushing my chair back into place or even about placing the books back on their proper shelves. I needed to get the hell out of there, out of that town.

If I was drunk before, I wasn't anymore.

The drive home was winding, every few feet having to avoid big balls of human-head sized snow flying from every direction. The Bronco rumbled through the thick ice and sleet, weaving through slicked roads and grassy fields hidden in a blanket of white. Whipping through the fields leaving dirty slushed tire tracks revealing the mud and dirt underneath. I made it to my mother's house across town in less than five minutes, leaving a trail of destruction behind me. I couldn't shake the feeling that something unknown was watching me, waiting on my every move, hoping for the right moment to snatch me up and send me into eternal hellfire.

My mother's small farmhouse glistened like the candles in the town windows. But the closer I arrived, the slower the Bronco drove, inching in slow motion toward the house like two magnets in the heavy air. It was as if a force stronger than my two-thousand-pound Bronco stopped me on the road, keeping me away from the house.

From my peripheral I saw a silver sedan skirt around the corner of the road and blast down the street, stopping abruptly in front of Mom's house and blowing tufts of snow and gravel through the tires. It took me a moment, but after rubbing my eyes I saw who it was. Seeing her must have broken the force in the wind, and the Bronco drove steadily up the driveway. I hopped out of the truck with it still running, my heart pumping a million miles a second.

"Stella?" I called, running up to the sedan. "Where have you been all day?"

WHAT'S ROTTING
UPSTAIRS

Stella's lengthy arms wrapped around my shoulders, and I held her like that for what seemed like an eternity. Breathing her in was a welcomed embrace that felt long overdue. She smelled of pine and poppies, a familiar scent that somehow smelled sweeter and more fragrant on her than anywhere else. I wanted to hold her forever.

"I'm so sorry about last night," she whispered into my ear, her red lips leaving a stain on my lobe. "I was totally stressed about the feast tonight and Sankta Lucia tomorrow. It's a big day—I just wanted it to be perfect."

"You're perfect." I kissed her on the forehead and pulled her in tighter, pausing time for just a moment before grabbing her hand and leading her inside. I didn't even care that the house was a mess, and the rotting opossum carcass still stained the bathroom floor upstairs. Our reunion felt more important.

We sat on the couch across from one another, staring into each other but trying to mask our endless smiles. It was like we were a couple of teenagers again, experiencing the tingles of love for the first time and not knowing how to speak about it. We stared so long our minds intertwined and connected into one being, one subconscious. It was as if she was *inside* my mind.

Stella let go of my hands and climbed on my lap, wrapping herself around me again. Her lips grazed my neck, softly brushing up against my skin; her breath rippling across the standing hairs on my body. She was feral, huffing and puffing like a lion, and I was her prey. Sharp teeth bit into my skin and pulled, like she couldn't resist the potency of the meat inside. I winced at the pain but sucked it in, embracing Stella's aggression. But still my mind was in a fog, hypnotized by her movements, and something came out of me that I didn't expect.

"*Stanisława,*" I moaned, the name coming from thin air as if I hadn't even said it myself, like it was pulled from inside of me. Stella, at hearing the word, instantly released her mouth from my neck and backed away, removing herself from my lap. She tilted her head like a curious dog, opening her lips to speak a few times before anything came out.

"Why did you call me that?" She mumbled something under her breath, looking confused. "I don't ever call you by names you don't want to be called, *Franciska.*"

"No need to be defensive, Stell. I don't know where that even came from—I guess I just *assumed.*" I grabbed her waist, hoping she'd let me lead her back to my lap, but she held strong, not moving an inch. "C'mon, it's not a big deal, is it?"

Her eyes cut into me like razor blades, a strong, almost evil face I didn't think someone like Stella could even possess. She was cold again, like how she'd looked the other night in the car. The glimmer in her eyes was gone, and they turned to flat black.

"It's not. But only my family calls me that." She smiled, but I knew it was fake. She winked at me, tickling my arm. "I was just surprised to hear that name coming from your mouth, that's all. Let's just forget it. Pretend it never happened."

The way she could push me away then suck me back into her trap within seconds made my stomach turn. In the days that we'd spent together, all I could think about was how perfect she was. How a life with her would look. How I *needed* her. But the uncertainty of Stella—the way she went up and down so quickly—churned like thick butter in my chest. I didn't want to be under her spell any longer, but every time I tried to push the thoughts of her away, the stronger and stronger they became. She had infiltrated me again, but I was still in there—somewhere. The coincidences hadn't fooled me completely.

"Hey Stella," I said, tickling her arm back, "since we're getting to know each other better—you never told me your birthday."

"Why, you gonna buy me a present?" She got closer, her hands on my waist, smiling, unsuspecting, exactly where I wanted her. "It's October twenty-fourth, right before my favorite holiday—besides *Lucia*."

I swallowed a boulder in my throat that sank to the bottom of my stomach and sat there, pushing all the acids up my esophagus. I dwelled in the burn for a while before catching my breath to speak, but nothing came out. Suspicion melted into my bones, leaking into the confusion that already resided in the connective tissue and mixed together into a chaotic mental concoction. I couldn't lose her, not like this, not after finding each other again and not to some stupid folktale or some random names on a weird list of nothing. My mind was playing tricks on me.

I pulled her in, not allowing my selfish immature fears to consume me. Nothing could disrupt what Stella and I shared. Not time, not space, not *anything*.

Except for Zula, who came creaking her tattered body into the living room from nowhere. She rubbed her coarse fur across my leg, sharp enough to poke through my jeans and scrape against my skin. Her old voice box croaked out a meow, broken and raspy but insistent. Her begging could only mean that hunger boiled in her belly, and she wouldn't let up until I fed her whatever was left in the bin under the sink.

Zula inhaled her cat kibble like she hadn't eaten in days. But I knew what was rotting upstairs. I knew just how abundant her meals had been in my absence, even if I wasn't the one to serve them. And still, my responsibilities as a new cat mother distracted me enough to forget that we weren't alone; someone was watching us from the couch, now inching closer and closer to remind me of their incessant importance.

Stella walked with soundless steps over to the kitchen and surprised me from behind, draping her arms around me and kissing my neck. My blood curdled at her touch, but I still welcomed it. My gut knew it was stupid, but my brain couldn't shake the images of her and I's future. Her love still contained me in its locked box, no matter how hard I tried to break free. I was just being paranoid. Anxious. My suspicions were only in my head.

"I need to grab something from the car," she whispered into my ear. "Don't miss me too much while I'm gone."

She glided through the back kitchen door, and when she shut it behind her I was at ease. My stomach settled for the first time in days. My mind released me of the constant images of her and I in bliss. Normally I'd never fall for someone so quickly, so impulsively. I'd always taken my time, gotten to know them, just to decide they were too this, too that, too *not for me*. With Stella I found that everything was perfect, just as it was when we'd first met. So then why did she suddenly make me so uneasy?

She swung the creaky door open, and it slammed against the kitchen counters, shaking the cabinets and knocking over the bin of almost-empty cat food, spilling the remains on the dirty tile. She held some sort of garment bag, slung over her forearm with that same fake smile plastered on her lips.

"I've got something for you," she said, enthralled. "You're gonna love it."

"What is it?" My voice was shaky, just as were my hands.

"Try it on, silly." Her hand touched my shoulder, and I backed away, unintentionally but subconsciously. "You're going to look *incredible*."

The bag was heavier than expected when Stella placed it carefully into my arms, like it contained a precious heirloom or something that couldn't dare be wrinkled. Habit had me walking toward the stairs to my mother's bathroom, but flashes of the stripped bones of the decaying opossum on the floor caught me and turned me around to the small guest bathroom on the main level.

Unzipping my jeans, I flung them on the floor along with my sneakers and t-shirt. The bag of spices fell from my pocket as it hit the tile floor, and I quickly stuffed it into my bra for safekeeping. I hung the garment bag from the hook on the door and unzipped it, revealing a black jeweled gown in very expensive looking fabric.

I hadn't worn something so elegant ever in my life, and I was unsure how to dress myself in all the bits and pieces in the bag. The buttery fabric of the satin gloves enticed my fingertips, a feeling that clothing had never brought me. Certainly nothing like the scratchy dresses my mother used to make me wear for church. Struggling to fasten the gold necklace I found in a jewelry box at the bottom of the bag, I walked out of the bathroom with the garment bag draped across my shoulder. I felt like an idiot.

"Are you sure all of this is necessary?"

When my head finally turned from the clothes on my body to the kitchen in front of me, I caught the sight of Stella, more enchanting than I'd ever seen before. In the few minutes that I was in the bathroom, she had somehow transformed herself, swathed in a long crimson off-the-shoulder evening gown, her black hair dressed in pin curls and adorned with a winter berry fascinator. Her dark lips that matched her dress parted into a dreamy smile as she opened her arms to me and helped me clasp my necklace. Forgetting my suspicions, I was hooked again.

"How did you get ready so fast?" I asked, but Stella put her fingers gently on my lips, shushing me before she kissed me, stealing all of my inquiries right from my hazed head. She wiped my mouth of her lipstick with her thumb, but I wanted to hold on to it forever. How quickly she could make me forget the strange coincidences, but I no longer cared about the silly history books and their tall tales.

"Come on," she purred into my warm ear, "we're gonna be late."

THE FEAST

Stella towered over me in her heels, her long sturdy legs strong enough to stop the whole world from crumbling. Nothing compared to my stumps. My ankles turned even whiter as we stood outside in the courtyard awaiting our entrance to the feast.

The old stone church at the top of the mountain stood there for hundreds of years, built by the hands of the Polish immigrants who began the traditions of Kolbe, the gray stone structure never having changed in all that time.

Cars piled up in the parking lot, filling the wintry courtyard with the bustle of voices and excitement. Garland with deep red berries, just like the ones in Stella's hair, decorated the wrought iron railing on the cement steps, and white tea light candles in red glass covers lined the entrance, flickering in the approaching night. We waited outside for what felt like an hour, freezing in the gusts before the massive wooden cathedral doors opened wide, inviting us into the celebration in the sanctuary.

The pews were pushed to the side, covered in white linen and artificial red poppies that made room for the giant table, spanning the length of the church, starting a few feet from the doors and ending all the way by the pulpit. Wooden folding chairs with more white linen and poppies lined the table, enough for the entire town.

Everyone in town was at the feast—my new favorite waitress, Jeannine, dressed in a forest green ball gown that matched the beads on her glasses string, and Mr. Ostrowski in a white tuxedo, gliding across the polished concrete floors with a fancy wooden cane, complete with a carved cobra head handle. The table was set with a long black satin runner, lined with pinecones and poppies and even more candles. It was as if we were attending a debutante ball at the decrepit cathedral, a dark gothic setting to usher in the festival of lights that would be brought with the morning sun. But for now, we celebrated the night.

Mr. Ostrowski made his rounds through the church, greeting the attendees of the feast as they came through the gusts from the massive doors. Stella clung to my hand, and we stood in the same place, like we were waiting for something to happen, not speaking a word to anyone around us. It was just as well; I barely knew anybody in town anymore, and I wasn't much for socializing. It was a miracle I was even convinced to appear at the feast, my suspicions having almost destroyed everything I had with Stella. But still her hand felt cold wrapped around mine, and the lack of greeting from anyone in the room was haunting.

"Exactly who I've been looking for!" Mr. Ostrowski hobbled his short frame back around to where Stella and I were standing, waving toward us. A rumble of light thunder crackled outside as he inched his way closer to us, joyous as ever to be reunited at such an occasion. "Come, Franciska, take your seat."

He led me to the largest chair at the head of the table, a throne meant for royalty. It couldn't possibly have been meant for me. But when he pulled the decorated throne from its spot at the end of the table, right in front of the pulpit, and motioned his hand for me to sit, I did. Stella sat at the other end of the table, all the way by the front doors a million miles from my presence. The others trickled in, taking their places across the lengthy table and hushing up at the sound of Mr. Ostrowski clinking his wine glass.

"I'd like to thank you all for coming tonight to the annual Feast of Saint Lucy," he spoke to the room of eager townsfolk, projecting across the sanctuary and echoing back and forth off the walls. "We've celebrated in this very church year after year, decade after decade—as far back as before some of you may remember. Our traditions have never left us, even as the world moves on and things inevitably change. We've remained true to our beliefs, and true to ourselves, which is why our strength as a community has stayed true all these years. But tonight is … not a normal night. As you all know, we've recently lost one of our own—an important part of our community. But we haven't gathered here tonight to wallow in our grief or turn this occasion into something that it's not. Because the truth is—there *is* beauty to be found in the darkness we've been forced to overcome. And sometimes, that beauty takes shape in the form of an old friend. Someone who you thought you'd never see again, but who came back to visit just in time. Tonight, we gather here not just for our regular festivities, but to celebrate our guest of honor—Miss Franciska Bosko, whose beloved mother Lucja is the reason this feast became a tradition in this town. I'm proud to be here with all of you in honor of the most magnificent woman this town has ever seen, and although it's been terrible having to let her go, having Franciska back is like having a piece of her again. So please, raise your glasses and let us make a toast to our guest, Franciska, and to the late, great, Lucja Bosko. To Lucy!"

"To Lucy!" The crowd cheered, glasses clinking together in memory of my mother, who I hadn't realized had made such an impact on the people of Kolbe. How could I forget the sleepless nights making saffron bread and biscuits, preparing for Sankta Lucia and the legendary feast the night before? How did I let go of such a vital part of my childhood, brushing it under the rug and sealing it tight with years of repressed memory?

Drink your tea, it'll help you to forget …

My grandmother introduced the tradition of Sankta Lucia to Kolbe, but it was my mother who brought the people together, my mother who made the townsfolk feel warm and trusting, and my mother who cultivated the traditions that stood the test of time, long beyond the religious aspects of the holiday. Kolbe was obsessed with the feast, and obsessed with the festival of lights, merely because my mother told them to be. Her influence traveled outside of our little farmhouse and into the town, her controlling manner was seen as kind and helpful, when removing the context of compassion and motherly nature. The same reasons I left this town and walked away from my mother's demands were the same reasons the town adored her.

"And now that we've paid our respects and welcomed young Franciska, here," Mr. Ostrowski continued, "Let us eat!"

The crowded room of townsfolk cheered, a symphony of joyous voices cackling and smiling in awe at the occasion. The people and their cheers seemed to be in sync, like a united group of like-minded folks, excited to dress up and eat a nice meal with their friends and neighbors. It was uplifting if not a little concerning. Their eyes all looked the same, too: black and empty, like their laughter and joy came not from within a body that contained a human soul but rather it was produced. I glanced at Stella, who was glancing back at me, unphased by the eruption of voices. In my most insecure of moments, I could always count on her to ease my pounding heart, even from hundreds of feet away from me on the other side of the longest ever table.

Men in all black uniforms and aprons carried large metal cloches in their gloved hands, placing them gently onto the table before lifting the lids and taking a small, synchronized bow. Lavishly decorated serving dishes full of kapusta, four different types of pierogi, stuffed cabbage, and the biggest pile of kielbasa I'd ever laid my eyes on graced the table, the scent of tarragon, fennel leaves, and thyme wafting through the air. Beautiful women proceeded into the sanctuary wearing white gowns with red sashes, a play on the traditional Sankta Lucia procession attire, holding silver platters containing comically large wine glasses with long stems, filled with blood red pinot noir.

The surrounding guests dug in at precisely the same moment, shoveling piles of the first course onto their plates and scarfing it down like they were feral animals, starved and malnourished. Even Stella was face down in a plate of potato and cheese pierogi, using her hands and the pierog dough to scoop up the kapusta and cabbages, ripping chunks out of the kielbasa with her pointy canines. Sipping my wine, I observed the rabid animals destroy their meals, mostly impressed at how quickly they could ingest it all.

The wine was stronger than expected, every sip warmed my belly and tingled my toes, soothing the nerves that wouldn't sit still. But the taste—I'd never had anything like it. A dark red that presented itself as dry and perhaps bitter, was sweeter than expected, rich with a strong flavor of differing ingredients, almost as if it wasn't a wine at all but a concoction brewed from home. Either way, it was delicious, intoxicating. I asked one of the women in white—who was walking around the table—for another glass, which prompted the feast-goers to all look at me in unison, noticing I hadn't eaten anything yet and scrunching their brows at the sight.

"Eat up, Franciska," Mr. Ostrowski boasted from the other end of the table, next to Stella, "we don't want our guest of honor leaving here skinny and unfed, do we?"

The others stared at me with their black empty eyes, taunting me with their persistence. Even the few elderly folks at the table were keen on intimidation, their big black irises shooting daggers in my direction. Shame poured over me and stuck to my skin, exposing my bareness to the whole town. I had offended them by not eating the food they'd prepared in my honor, a phenomenon I hadn't had to think about since leaving the confines of my cultural home. Nobody in the city cared if I even lived or died, let alone if I'd finished my supper.

Mr. Ostrowski chuckled under his breath, followed by an eruption of cackling from the table. The whole town of Kolbe screamed, doubled over, and pounded the table with fists of uncontrollable laughter that rang through their whole bodies. Mothers, sisters, and old men, convulsing like something had slipped into their drinks, triggering some sort of mass hysteria. They sloshed mounds of pierogi and kapusta and kielbasa onto a plate, passing it from person to person until the food piled into a mountain peak, toppling over when the last person slammed the plate in front of me, insisting with his head nods and eager smile that I gobble it up for everyone to see.

I scanned the table, and everyone was staring at me, waiting for me to indulge. Even Stella and her piercing goldish eyes lingered over me with anticipation. I cut a bite off of the kielbasa with my fork and shoved it in the hole, my teeth ripping the meat apart in my mouth. But the table wasn't satisfied, they sat in silence still as they watched me intently, hoping for some sort of changed outcome. The next fork full was an entire pierog—slathered in sour cream and topped with kapusta—much too big for one bite but hopefully enough for the prying eyes. I swallowed it whole, hot potatoes and cheese melting in my throat and burning my esophagus. But once it had settled in my gut, the table quickly switched back to the loud joyous energy it had before, silverware scraping against the fine China, friends laughing and gushing about the night ahead.

"More wine?" Another young woman in white startled me, tapping me on the shoulder from behind. I hadn't realized I already finished my second glass, but I wasn't in any position to refuse. I held my glass out, letting her pour the dark berry liquid all the way until it reached the top of my glass. *A heavy pour for a heavy heart, right?*

The liquid inside the chalice of a wine glass sploshed around as I carefully dragged it across the table toward me, making desperate attempts at not spilling a drop on the shiny white tablecloth. My face instinctually lowered to the glass to slurp a little off the top, a habit leftover from childhood. But I quickly straightened up, remembering how I was taught to act while dressed in fancy clothes, pretending I was some sort of intellectual. Out of place in the most elegant dinner I'd ever been invited to, implied ridicule trickled into my bones through the looks on everyone's faces.

One shaky sip and my belly was on fire.

A second sip and my blood vessels restricted, tightening my skin around the muscles underneath.

A third and the room became blurry, people's heads wobbling off their necks and swaying back and forth.

A final gulp and the glass was empty, my loose fingers twirling it around in my hand until it fell from my weightless fingertips, smashing onto the ground below. Glass flew in a million directions and danced around the room as they floated down to the floor. My neck slowly guided my head around the table, the guests' faces all melting into one ominous creature.

Warped laughter invaded my already ringing ear drums; they throbbed and pulsed like buzzing bees were fighting death within the canals.

The unified town creature laughed harder and harder as the flickering lights swallowed the room whole, overwhelming the blurred image of light and movement and color until it faded away altogether.

"Whaaat.. uss... haaa... pen.. ung...?" I tried to spill the words from my lips, but everything was slow. Hazy. Slipping ... away.

And then it was black.

LUCY

"Let's go, Franciska." My mother sighed, tapping the points of her high-heeled shoes. "We're going to be late."

I wiggled my hand into the open sleeve of my dark wool coat and rushed out to the front entrance, Zula two steps behind me, hunting for my ankles. I knew we wouldn't actually be late, because the party couldn't start without my mother. Her presence was an intoxicating force to the townspeople who looked up to her.

"I'm ready, Mama," I huffed, struggling to catch my breath.

My mother's old station wagon raced with the snowstorm outside, windshield wipers doing their best but leaving icy lines behind on the glass. The feast was my least favorite part of Sankta Lucia, a magical night of lights and warm sentiment. The feast on December twelfth was a cold and stuffy tradition, like everyone in the room was only there to judge my every move. But I never refused, mostly because it made my mother happy. Her smile glowed in the lights of the candles that filled the sanctuary of the old Kolbe Church house.

We always arrived at the celebration early, a condition of the responsibility put upon my mother by herself, a self-appointed leadership role in which she nitpicked every little detail of the feast's decor, schedule, even the number of candles placed around the room. Her dedication to a party that only happened once a year was impressive if not a little intimidating. Nobody would dare cross her, annoy her, or interrupt her during Sankta Lucia preparations or the planning of the feast; it wouldn't possibly end well for them if they tried.

"Roland, fix these place settings," she snapped at a shorter, slightly older man.

"Jeannette, fix your hair, it looks ridiculous!" A young woman with large pink glasses and a matching velvet gown walked away with her head hanging low.

My mother's power loomed over the night, and it hadn't even begun. The other people helping in the church rushed around the room, scrambling to make ends meet in a manner that was acceptable to her. Outside, the sky blackened in contrast to the bright white snow falling a million miles a second. Large chunks of ice crashed against the stained-glass windows, but the townsfolk, doomed to help set up the evening's festivities, couldn't be bothered with the weather; the feast was the only thing of importance.

Watching from a small chair tucked into a hidden corner of the pulpit was the only enjoyment I'd find from the evening. As a small child I'd already figured out that religious holidays weren't exactly my cup of tea, and staying up all night to eat Polish food (which I ate every day anyway) wasn't as exciting as the adults had made it seem. Dressing up in an ugly puffy dress to sit and watch the people I'd known my whole life pretend they'd adopted some sort of elegance overnight was excruciating to me. But regardless of the religious aspects, at least Sankta Lucia was full of light, full of hope. The feast felt like the darkest night of the year and not just because it actually *was* one of the darkest nights of the year.

"You can wait here, but *don't you dare* mess up your outfit," she said before joining her friends for a glass of wine over by the organ.

An aging priest eyed me from the small window in the sacristy door, pointing to a piece of saffron bread and then pointing back to me. I nodded, understanding his hand signals. Instantly the squeaky door swung open, and the priest appeared with a plate of bread and ginger cookies. He walked in staggered stomps to place the dish on my lap, using his hand to bless the treat with the sign of the cross. I ravaged the bread and cookies, having not eaten all day as my mother nearly drove herself to a heart attack worrying about the feast. Crumbs and chunks of slobbery food landed all over my satin dress, something that would've risked further panic from my mother had she seen. The priest pulled out his handkerchief, dusting the mess from my clothing and the corners of my lips.

"What's a young lady like you doing in this old dusty church so late at night?" His Polish accent comforted me like a piece of home, a piece of my family. I giggled, knowing the old priest knew exactly why I was there. He also knew exactly who my mother was. Everybody in town knew Lucy Bosko, even if they didn't want to. "You're in the procession tomorrow night, aren't you? You should be getting your beauty sleep tonight!"

He winked at me, ruffling up my hair with his wrinkly hands, to which I promptly brushed back into place with my fingers, not wanting my mother to see me disheveled on her big night. He started to walk away, but curiosity got the better of me.

"Hey mister?" I asked, tugging at the back of his black priest's gown. "Why's everybody care about this feast so much?"

"Well," he chuckled, "mostly because people like to have something to look forward to. But sometimes, when the moon is hidden behind the storm clouds, the glow disappearing into the night, I shiver to think something *evil* lives behind those clouds."

My little legs trembled, and my palms moistened. My heart raced in incomplete pumps: staggered and unnatural. My lungs locked my breath into my chest, holding it hostage as my eyes widened. Unknowingly, my fingers again gripped the priest's cassock, tightening until the knuckles turned white.

"Do you ..." A gasp of breath spilled from my throat and shook my vocal cords as I struggled to speak. "Do *you* think there's evil here in Kolbe?"

"Evil lives in the dark, my dear, when little girls like you should be asleep, lost in a fairytale of dreams. Evil lives in the neighbors you know, and the doors they close behind them. Sometimes it lives in the people you know the best. It's in the roaring wind and the raging blizzards that come from somewhere only the devil himself knows. Storms in this town don't come for no reason, my child. *The storms only come when evil is behind them.*"

Releasing my fingers from his vestment, I covered my eyes with my sweaty hands, leaving a crack between fingers for me to peek through. The thick tights that my mother made me wear were scratching at my skin, leaving microscopic tears on the top layer on my shins. The priest sat on the pulpit ledge beside me, leaning into me, and drawing the cross over my forehead with tightly closed fingers. Reaching into a pocket on the side of his black robe, he pulled out a tiny red pull string bag with something fragrant wafting from inside.

"What is that?" I said, pulling off the shield from my face.

The priest grabbed my hands, placing the red bag in my palms, and closing my fingers around it. His glossy eyes stared intently into mine, bulging at the seams of his eye sockets.

"This will keep you safe. From evil and anything else." His shaking fingers gripped even tighter, squeezing my wrists until they were red and bulging. "Promise me you won't fall into their trap—promise me you'll protect yourself from evil!"

Ripping my hands from his grasp, I ran to find my mother but not before stashing the bag in between the bow in my dress ribbon for safekeeping. I couldn't be sure that the priest wasn't telling the truth.

I found Mom dancing around the organ, surrounded by other towns-people, sloshing their wine glasses and laughing hysterically. I fell into her, wrapping my small arms around her waist as she towered over me in her sparkly green dress and gold heels, a matching gold crown affixed on her dusty blonde tendrils—emanating the Queenhood that she possessed, in all the night's glory.

"Dance with me," she whispered, kissing the top of my head and pulling me closer to her. My face pressed deep into her stomach as we swayed back and forth, my tears seeping into her dress but hiding behind the shininess of the sequins attached. Her power wasn't always used for bad—to keep me and others under her spell. Sometimes it was used to comfort, to protect. Her energy that fed off of everyone else who dared to be in her presence, would also feed the whole town—feed the entire world if she could. My mother was my mother, and I couldn't change her. And sometimes, I didn't want to. "Dinner should be ready soon. Would you like to see the special seat I prepared for my special girl?"

"Sure!" I wasn't very hungry anymore after eating so much saffron bread and ginger cookies. But I wanted to see what had been created from the magic of my mother's delegating. I was impressed with how beautiful the night was put together, all from ideas that were born in that mysterious head of hers. Even as her own child, I'd never been able to read my mother, and whenever I tried, it was as if my thoughts were blocked. But despite my insistence of the contrary, I was always interested in what she had to say.

Pulling a shiny white cloth from a large chair placed at the head of the table, my mother revealed the throne she had acquired for the evening, that was apparently meant to seat me. Tall wooden rails held the massive throne, detailed with intricate carvings into the wood, depicting a forest mountain scene, with deep green velvet cushions fit for the butt of a king.

"You're our special guest this evening," my mother said, smiling and waving her arm at the throne like she was the beautiful cohost of a game show, taunting me with my potential prize. "Sit!"

The velvet cushion brushed against the satin skirt, cushioning my bottom in a bed of shiny clouds. The long hand carved legs held me up higher than any of the other chairs at the table, like I really was a king looking down on the commoners. Once I was seated, the others started to file in, taking their seats and unfolding their cloth napkins onto their laps. My mother sat at the other end of the table, like a Queen, in a smaller but just as intricately carved throne—adorned with blood red velvet cushions.

A man in a fancy black tuxedo rang a large bronze bell, prompting a line of equally well-dressed men with white gloves carrying silver platters with large domed cloches to the table. In unison they placed them in front of us, lifting the cloches and revealing the meal, before taking a bow and exiting stage left. A meal fit for a Polish King was presented for our eyes to feast upon—red barszcz served with porcini uszka, herring and gołąbki, kutia and different types of pierogi. My mouth watered at the sight. My mother was the first to go, plating a bit of everything and passing the dish 'round the table until it was placed in front of me. Once I'd taken my first bite, the others followed suit, piling food onto their fancy plates and passing it around the table until everyone had a serving.

I ate until the waistband on my itchy white tights tried to escape from their threads, stretching the elastic with my fist under the table so nobody would see, and laying back in my throne. The food fatigue crept up behind my eyeballs and sent cold sweats down my body and through my pores. But before I could retreat to the confines of the covered pews, waiting for my mother to be finished with her duties of the night so we could finally go back home, she insisted I finish my tea. I hadn't noticed the gold teacup being served to me in my devouring of the meal, but I drank it up in one large gulp, wanting to please my mother. But as soon as the warm liquid traveled down my throat and into my belly, the sleepiness overwhelmed the blood pumping from my heart, and I began to fade away ...

I awoke to the biting wind scraping against my unclothed skin. The world was dark, except for a glowing in the distance. Strange, hooded figures carried my naked body toward the light, crunching their feet on the snow below them. No stars twinkled in the sky, only blackness looming over me, and I was unable to make out any faces in the dark.

We arrived at the glowing light, which I could now see was a raging fire built from an unusual arrangement of twigs and pine branches, sprinkled with what looked like herbs and dried flower petals placed in a circle surrounding the fire. My breathing quickened to short abrupt breaths, but I tried to conceal my fear, for it seemed to motivate the robed figures even more. Through the light from the fire, I could make out the peaks of the mountains around us, but they were no longer tipped with ice caps of fresh snow, but blanketed in a dark crimson ooze, like the rocks themselves were bleeding.

The creatures brought me to the fire, raising me high in the sky above it, and tying my hands and feet to four stakes in the ground with rope. I laid there, suspended in air and smelling the fuzzy hairs on my back burning in the fire. My body started to heat up, like one of those extra hot sunny days when I would stay out too long, and my skin would burn to a crisp. I was sure I was toast, ready to turn into crunchy bacon to be devoured by whatever *thing* had brought me to the fire. But just as I was ready to die out there in the mountains, something that looked to be twenty feet tall slithered their way to me with incredible speed, like a snake on steroids.

When it made its way to me and the fire, the crowd of hooded figures began to chant something, starting slow and soft but increasing in volume and intensity the more they chanted. The smoke coming from the fire clouded the group of chanting figures, concealing them as they grabbed one another's hands and danced around the fire. The giant creature began to contort their body in unnatural ways, crawling to me like a possessed being—some sort of demon or monster. My heart raced and sweat dripped from my brow into the fire, making a sizzling sound as it hit the flames. The creature got closer and closer to me, until it was right in front of my face, breathing cold breath onto my neck. It pulled off its hood, revealing its face, which confused me even more.

"Mama," I said, still unsure of what I was seeing but able to recognize her eyes anywhere. She opened her mouth, unveiling thousands of sharp teeth, saliva raining from her gums as she got closer and closer. "Mama, no!"

But something distracted her, taking her gaze away from my beating heart. In a swift motion, another robed creature coming from nowhere in the night grabbed at my wrist, dragging me away from the fire through the freezing snow. My head clonked against hundreds of small little rocks and bumps on the ground, until my useless vision blurred to swirls and sparkles, and then nothing at all.

My eyes shot open, and I was back in my twin size bed, back in the comfort of my bedroom inside a puddle of sweat. My mother came through the door, carrying a cup of steaming tea and smiling. She sat down at the edge of my comforter, smelling of flowers and safety. She brushed my soaked hair from my eyes, kissing me on the forehead.

"I'm so sorry you're still having these nightmares, my love," she whispered. She motioned for me to sit up, offering me the cup with a hand towel wrapped around the base, shielding me from burning my hands as she handed me the soothing liquid. "Drink your tea, now, darling. It'll help you to forget."

THE FEEDING

My throbbing ear drums faded in and out of rustling noises. Whooshes of abrupt sound whirling through my head, cut short by the muffled plugs of freezing air. Bursts of warm breath huffed over my body in sporadic waves, coming from all directions to bite my numbing skin. My eyelids were too heavy to open, glued shut and the lashes intertwined into a tangled spider web, sealing the cracks. Even the thoughts inside were shadowed by blackness surrounding.

My chest rose and fell in small increments, restricted by a sharp pain that appeared every time I attempted a deep breath. The veins under my skin were so tightly bound within my body I thought they might burst, spilling out all of my life's force. Even my heart pumped with less voracity and strength than before, locked and tightened in its cage within my ribs and sheltered lungs.

Crisp biting air hit my nose hairs, freezing them on contact. Cheap church candles burned in the distance, the smoke a familiar tale of plastic-y wax and warmth. Something sweet tickled my taste buds, connecting to scent, remembering the flowery wine that lingered on my tongue. *How long ago had I drunken it?* The only clear thought I could muster.

Footsteps became apparent as my senses cleared, footsteps that crunched and rustled above whatever land lived below. My wrists burned like they'd been rubbed raw, the skin pounded into dust and flaking off with every movement of my numb hands.

My ankles suffered the same burning sensations as my wrists, my ribs hiding inside myself, not letting any air through, trying to not meet the same fiery fate as my limbs. My entire body was tightened beyond comfortability, entrapped within the confines of invisible restraints. *If only I could open my damn eyes …*

Hints and glimmers of many different whispering voices hovered around me, a constant mumbling lingering in the atmosphere. No longer allowing the heaviness of my eyelids to prevent me from inspecting my new surroundings, I forced myself to rip them open, tangled lashes falling off in clumps, a casualty of circumstance.

My eyes were opened but my sight was useless; blurry shadows and smeared streaks of black soot blocked any sort of understanding of the scene. *What the hell was happening to me?* I blinked quickly to clear my vision. My wrists and ankles were tied to a metal grate by thick rope that had by now rubbed my skin raw. Blood was smeared all up and down my arms and legs, like I'd been fighting with the shackles that bound me.

Something brushed against my leg, the texture of loose fabric grazing my exposed ankles. A whispered gasp followed, and then the glowing golden eyes that latched onto mine for only a mere millisecond stung a deeper part of my recognition. A familiar floral musk clung to the hairs in my nostrils, calming me but confusing me even more.

"Stella?" I spoke into the void. I was hoping the void would answer back. "Stella is that you?"

The rustling stopped, as did the crunching of snow around me. The world was frozen in time again, until my ears picked up on faint voices, croaking little voices—near me but far away at the same time.

"She wasn't supposed to wake up yet."

"She wasn't supposed to wake up *at all*."

"This is going to ruin everything!"

"No, we just have to do this now, before it's too late."

Thunder crashed and lightning soon followed, illuminating the void and revealing the massive Babia Mountains. The blue rocks looked gray and decaying, the ice capped peaks melted into a rusty crimson, viscous and runny, bloody like my body. Thunder roared again but the lightning stayed quiet, the sky instead pouring down buckets of sharp snow, piercing my skin and blocking my view of the bleeding Babias.

Another burst of cackling sky and the peaks of the mountains disappeared as I was lowered in the air, movement ceasing as I'd apparently made it to my final resting place. *This feels familiar somehow*—but I still couldn't see what I was looking at, the snow had picked up tenfold. Something howled in the sky; I looked and found the moon was full and crimson too, swollen with blood waiting to burst from the craters.

A spark cracked and fire ignited all around me in a circle. The smell of fennel leaves and marjoram, thyme and tarragon, wafted with the swirling wind, fooling my senses and encouraging a growling in my stomach. But I wasn't there to eat; the feast had already ended for me. I was there to be *eaten*; as I always had been in my nightmares as a child. This was all just a dream; it *had* to be.

I just needed to wake up.

Wake up and drink my tea.

And then I could forget ...

The fire created heat on my ripped gown, sweat dripping into my wounds and stinging the exposed meat inside. Strange cackling voices raged louder and louder, closer and closer to me, but the snow raged harder. And then the music started.

Sounds of the sixties and seventies rang through the air, stuff from my childhood and even before, stuff my mother used to play all the time, the kind of music she used to dance to in the kitchen wearing her long flowy dresses and floral scarves in her hair.

The fire flamed higher and finally melted some of the incoming snow; the glow was enough to see a few feet in front of me, enough to see the robed creatures crawling toward me, their bones cracking and ripping at the joints as their unhuman bodies raced to meet me at my fiery post. But instead of retching their bodies onto me, creeping their unnatural limbs up to greet my vulnerable body, they began to dance. Dance in waves around the circle of fire, their robes flowing in the wind. It reminded me of my mother, dancing around the stove when she cooked for me, her flowy dress frolicking along with her.

Flashes of the creatures' gray skin haunted me as they swayed offbeat to the music, erratic motions that somehow seemed rhythmic and synchronized. More thunder blasted on with the dancing, the lightning mimicking their movements. The heat from the fire began to boil my skin, bubbles forming at the seams of my wounds; the smell of pennies being cooked as the life spilled out from within me.

As the music lulled, preparing for the next song, the creatures screeched into the dark night, howling and cackling at the blood-filled moon, ready to burst and shower over us. I'd never gotten that far in the dream as a child; my mother always seemed to wake me up just at the right moment. But my cooking skin and boiling blood made me think that it wasn't a dream at all, I was really being cooked alive on the top of a damn mountain. *But where was my mother now?*

Scratching of a record screeched in the night and the music stopped, as did the dancing. The creatures all turned to look at me, smack dab in the center of the fire, alive but burning to a crisp. Their faces were still concealed by their hooded robes, but their glowing eyes pierced into me, dozens of them open wide and stuck on their target. The creatures snarled like rabid animals, salivating from all orifices. Their bodies twisted until their bones broke, dragging their unhinged limbs behind them as they crawled up through the fire and onto the giant barbecue grate that held me in place, slithering up like snakes. At least twenty rotten creatures hiding behind robes leaped from the ground and onto my melting skin, laughing and snarling as they sprinkled herbs and dried petals over me, stuffing some into my mouth and ears. My body screamed in pain with every dash of spices that were poured onto my disintegrating skin— inflamed with every fistful of herbs shoved into another cavity.

"Stop it, please!" I screamed at the creatures, spitting out the herbs onto my chest, but that only motivated them more. They cackled at the swollen moon until it finally burst open, pouring the bloody rain over the mountains until all of us—myself and the creatures—were slathered in it like barbeque ribs. The creatures became excited by the storm of thick blood, using their black textured tongues to lick it off of me, grunting as they did so. My stomach turned, and it took all of me not to vomit all over myself and the creatures. "No, no no no no!"

My screams must have meant something, stopping the creatures in their tracks, if only for a mere moment—

"That's enough!" A powerful voice louder than the thunder screamed from the heavens, prompting the creatures to scurry away, back to their positions around the fire. They waited in silence for their god to appear; I waited for something, anything, to change as my skin turned to burnt bacon. As lightning ripped through the sky, the creatures began to chant, stripping off their robes. They stood staring into space, naked and more human looking than I'd thought. Their chants started as a whisper, increasing in strength the louder the thunder roared.

"Lucja ..." *tap tap tap.*

"Lucja ..." *tap tap tap.*

"LUCJA!"

They howled and cheered and danced again, waving their gray arms in the air as they continued their chanting. The chanting of my mother's name.

And then she appeared.

Taller than the mountains and dripping blood, guts, and whatever else, she was on me in an instant. Her foaming mouth was ripped open and bleeding, allowing room for the thousands of teeth sticking out from her blackened gums in all sorts of crooked positions. Her skin was like leather, rippled and thick but melting away. She wasn't anything like I'd seen before, but I'd recognize the smell of poppies and her judgmental stare anywhere.

"Mama?" I cried, "how c-could this b-be?"

Her eyes widened, letting go of a salted tear that ran down to her neck. She fell onto me, her tears soothing my burning skin.

"I've missed you, my girl." Her arms wrapped around my neck, holding me tightly into her like she'd always done when I was a child. She smelled faintly of the flowers I'd always remembered, but mostly of rotted flesh and death. "I've been falling apart without you."

"I thought …" I was still in shock. "I thought you were dead."

"I was," my mother said, lifting herself from me to look me in the eyes, "in a way …"

"What do you mean?"

"You … you are the reason I still exist on this planet, the reason I can still breathe Earth's air." She turned her head away from me, looking around at her loyal servants circling her. "I've been *starving* without you, Franciska, and it's time we fix that, don't you think?"

Her followers surrounding us laughed in unison, cheering on their leader.

"What is all of this?" I asked, stupidly, not knowing how badly I did *not* want to know the answer. "Who are all these people?"

"Don't you recognize them?" She laughed, pointing down at the creatures below. "They're your friends and neighbors, can't you see?"

The creatures twisted their bodies around to face me all at once, smiling from ear to ear like they were possessed. The creatures weren't creatures at all but the townsfolk that I'd spent the last few days with. Jeannette from the diner stood there enthralled with her colorful glasses, standing next to other people

I'd recognized from brief encounters in town but didn't know personally. And when I panned my eyes to the left, I saw Mr. Ostrowski and his crooked teeth, smiling wide, holding hands with the one person I wish I'd never seen.

Stella, no, not you too ...

My mother had taken everything away from me, just as she'd always done. As a child I never had a sense of self, everything revolved around her and her ideas, her rituals, her frequent meltdowns at the slightest inconvenience. I never got to experience what it was like to be a normal kid, never got to run around town like a stupid teenager or make normal mistakes. I was condemned to my mother's wishes—born to serve her until the day I died.

That's why I had skipped out of Kolbe and never looked back. It wasn't the small-town loneliness or the single shared brain cell of the folks that lived there—it was *always* because of her. Her hold on me could only last as long as the law allowed, and there was nothing—besides a little cash and the promise of her death—that could've ever brought me back to that stupid little town in the middle of nowhere. And yet there I laid, frozen in time at the top of a mountain, bloody and ripped open, forced to reckon with the grip of my mother's cold dead fingers wrapped around my neck.

"Mom," I cried, "you need to let me go."

"No!" Her decaying fingers ripped off of my neck, arms flying into the air and casting a symphony of thunder and blizzarding snow to wash over the mountains. The ground below shook as gusts of biting wind raced back and forth, blowing the fire into bursts of flames and creating a twister of fire and snow and ... blood. The blood from the tips of the Babias gushed over me, dripping from the ropes that bound me, and raining into the fire, sizzling as it poured over the robed townsfolk.

They danced in the bloody rain and snow like true creatures of the night, opening their mouths and letting the wet sky trickle over their rotted teeth, guzzling it up like they'd been starving for it. Stella was especially excited for the delicious treat quenching her slithering tongue, moving her body in erratic jerks like she'd been served liquid gold. Inhale and exhale of hysterical laughter broke up the thunder and crackled louder than the flames. My skin was melting from the meat underneath, cooking from the smoke I inhaled, smelling of a medium rare steak. It wouldn't be long now before I was fully well done.

"I can't let you go, Franciska, why can't you see that?" My mother lowered her frail arms, and the storm calmed, her loyal sidekicks quieting down, waiting. Tears fell from her glowing eyes, and her face softened, if only for a moment. "You're all I've ever had, Franciska. My only child, my only life source. When you left town, it nearly killed me, did you know that? Did you know I cried myself to sleep for months and months, maybe even years? I've been lonely. *Starved* for your affection, hungry for reassurance that you'd be back one day. But I never got that reassurance, Franciska. All I got were unanswered calls and returned letters. But now you're here, now you can *feed my soul* again. How could I possibly let you go this time?"

Salty tears burned as they ran down my boiling skin. My mother had been confirmed dead for days—dead *to me* for a decade. But was her death all just a sick little trick of hers? A ploy to force me home and back into her good graces, just to punish me for having left in the first place? Punish me for my life *choices*—like who I loved or what clothes I wore. I was never meant to do things on my own, was I? My heart yearned for the loneliness of the city escape I'd cultivated, the break I'd had from the confines of my mother's grip.

"Mom, please, this isn't fair to me ..."

Habit and reflex kicked in and my arm raised to wipe the tears from my cheeks, ultimately stopped by the ropes that tied me to the scorching metal grate underneath my back. But a little tug of the wrist sent particles of frayed rope into the fire below, loosening the tie on my right side, opening the trap. If only I could do that again to the left side and then to both my ankles.

But as if she'd known my plans to escape all along, my mother fell on top of my crumbling chest, wrapping herself around me, and holding me in place. But she wasn't simply keeping me from running away nor was her rancid mouth merely dripping foam from her sharp teeth. She was sobbing, barely catching her breath as the storm of emotion rained into my wounds.

"What about what's fair to *me*?" She struggled to speak through her wails. "All I've ever wanted was to be closer to you. To teach you the ways of your own heritage, for you to be *proud* of it. If only you knew how much I've really protected you from, Franciska. How much I've hidden behind closed doors, just to make sure you'd be safe—here with me. But as soon as you found a little freedom, you abandoned me and left me in the dust to rot. You became someone I didn't even recognize, like I'd raised a complete stranger. I never would have been like those *other mothers* who abandon their children for choosing a different *lifestyle*. I would have tried to understand, but you never let me even try! You assumed the worst of me, and you pushed me away because of it. You left me here, alone. And I don't think you *ever* thought about what that's done to me. How could you do that to your *only* mother, Franciska?"

A phrase I'd heard a million times—the *how could you do this to me* game that plagued my childhood, filling my insides up with guilt for a life I'd never asked to live. The mind games may have kept me from ever crossing my mother in the past, but I'd learned a lot in the ten years I'd spent away from her.

I liked being alone, where my thoughts were my own and not hers.

MELTED GOO

Dark brown spittle flew from my mother's crusty lips as I rejected her manipulation. Her face hardened again, her eye sockets sunken and dark, the skin graying and wrinkling. Second by second, she began to resemble the version of her that lived in the morgue—decaying and cold. Her limbs twisted and cracked, crawling backwards with her head still faced toward me; her eyes were hooked with focused intent. Her voice began to change, too, deepening lower and lower into a distorted mess of demonic projection. Failing at her game of sympathy, she went back to her original plan of intimidation—*but that's just mama.*

"You took, and took, and *took* as a child, and then what do I get? An ungrateful brat who runs away the first chance she gets. Well not anymore, little girl. No, now it's time to give your *mommy* back some of what she deserves." She grew twenty feet in the air, a goliath of broken bones and decaying flesh, hovering over the night sky.

My muscles turned to buttery filet mignon, and the blood drained from the gashes in my limbs, weakening me with every drop that dripped into the soil of the Babias. Breathing through my nose kept my heart steady, necessary for not exerting too much energy.

But it wasn't good enough.

My eyelids weighed a thousand tons, and without my free hands to hold them open, I had no choice but to let them fall where they may, allowing the dark world to swallow me up and spit me into the depths of deadly hell. The mountains surrounding me wafted away into a black vignette, closing in tighter and tighter.

Small blips of vision cycled in and out as my eyelids fluttered between open and closed. It took all my strength to watch what was happening in front of me but failing, fading, slowly away. In my mind, my body, light as a budgie feather, drifted off into the dark sky, blood and guts and sprinkled with seasoning, flying into the night. But my brain wouldn't let me go, and the cracks in my lids revealed the true nature of the evening.

One by one the witches circling my failing body crawled on all fours to my metal coffin, unaffected by the fire that now roared past the bloody moon into space and beyond. Their skin, grayish blue, disintegrated into dust that fell off in flakes and sprinkled over me—a little extra seasoning for the feast they'd been preparing. Hearing was warped to drowned buzzing, pulsating through my temples and washing out the sounds of the creatures feasting.

Cold spiky tongues slobbered over my crisped skin and tugged at the smoked muscles in my legs. My mother took a special interest in watching this feast of demons, eyes peeled as they tore the loose flesh off my thighs with their sharp teeth. With every bite of my meat, the color rushed back to her face, brittle bones strengthened, and human features returned to her being.

"Look!" she yelled to her coven, "It's working! I'm returning! No longer is our coven in danger! Our powers of darkness will soon prevail!"

"Lucja! Lucja! Lucja!" The coven chanted my mother's name, pieces of my flesh hanging from their teeth and spit flying out of their gaping mouths.

"It's not over yet, though, I'm afraid." My mother spoke as a true leader, guiding her subjects through their own salvation. "We have to finish her, *all of her*, or the spell won't be complete."

Too weak to scream and too broken to try and kick them off of me, I accepted my fate, allowing the fire and ice to rip me open and melt my flesh, perfectly ripe for the slobbering feast. The animals ravaged through my body, working their way up from my feet and legs; whole chunks of myself torn from me and ripped apart by stabbing teeth. The crack in my eyelids tightened as my heart pumped slower, and slower, and slower …

In my defeat I loosened my bones that were clenched, giving in to my destiny as a warm meal for my mother's sickly friends. Laying into the burning poles, my arms fell backward, and with a crack and a few sparks of the flames they released into the snow and rock below, free from their shackles.

A surge of adrenaline raged through the few veins I still had intact as I realized my newfound autonomy. My eyes opened wide, awake and alive. I slowly moved my free hand to my chest, grasping the bag of oregano that I'd kept hidden in my bra all that time. How glad I was to find that silly little velvet pouch, something that seemed so insignificant just a day ago. It gave me comfort as I met my fate.

Through the slivers of sight I had left, a distant hint of pink in the sky glittered through the opening in the bloody mountains, pumping my blood with even more vitality. A hazy orange glow surrounded the ritual, illuminating my mother's servants as they made a mess of my parts. Time had been but a construct up there in the mountains; the dark had shadowed any semblance of the hours going by. The sneaky sun was starting to come up, the witches now in a race against the clock to complete their ritual in the ever-fading dark.

"Wait, Mama, please just listen to me for a second," I cried with shallow breath. "I'm sorry for everything. Please give me a chance to make it up to you. I don't want to be bad anymore, I promise. I'll do whatever you want."

My mother's head perked up, waving the witches away from my bloody body and floating up to meet my gaze. Her hands, soft and human, grazed my bubbling skin, resting gently on my neck.

"Words are sweet, my love, but your heart tastes even sweeter."

"I know you don't mean that," I said. The cracks in her soft skin began to form again, her gums fading from bubblegum pink to a rotten gray. Foam settled at the corners of her lips, salivating as my skin was smoked like a pig. The pinkish orange of the sky now cascaded up the mountains, inching closer and closer to final sunrise. I stayed calm and stroked my velvet pouch full of old oregano, only needing a few more minutes. "Your death shattered me into a million pieces, even if I wouldn't admit it. I was selfish for leaving you so vulnerable, and I regretted it every single day. I could never watch you die *again*, especially not after we finally found each other after all these years. I *know* that you spared me in the past, Mama. I know that deep down, you don't really want to do this. I just want to help you. There has to be another way, Mom. Another way where I get to have you in my life and me in yours. I don't want our reunion to end like this! What if ... what if I came back home to live with you?"

"Sweeter words have never been spoken." Her sharp teeth burst through her blackened mouth as she smiled, growing larger with each heavy breath she took, hovering over my dying body. She fell onto my chest, wrapping her decaying arms around me. "Unfortunately for you, there's no other way but through my *stomach*."

Her teeth clenched onto my side, ripping through the dermis like an apple peel, tearing through pounds of yellow slimy fat and slurping it up with her slithering tongue. Blood gushed from every direction, pouring out of me like a pitcher, spraying like a hose from my exposed ribs.

Now we both raced against the rising sun; her hunger grew with every second that passed, my body failing me with every millisecond. I didn't have any more time.

Holding my breath deep within my withering lungs, I angled my foot as much as the ropes would let me and pushed toward the heat from the flames where it burned and burned. Ashes of my charred skin and sparks of lit rope flew off into the Babias where they would lie until the mountains crumbled. I clenched my teeth until they broke apart, taking every rush of blood still left inside of me to stop myself from screaming in pain.

And with nothing left to lose and mere moments to survive, I flung the ropes from my ankles, catching a piece of the nearly molten metal that flew in the air as it ripped from the grate. Pieces of my skin and cooked meat went flying with the ropes, spreading human confetti over the deathly looking witches. The rising sun grew louder still, peaking at the tips of the mountains and threatening to illuminate the brightening sky. Clinging to my pouch full of herbs and releasing my breath from its chest prison, I took in a deep inhale, knowing it was all I had left.

"Looks like you're running out of time," I said, pushing my mother to the side where she rolled into the flames, her eyes glowing red as she stared at her only daughter's betrayal. "Guess you'll have to *starve* tonight."

As the sky cooled from a dusty orange to an ocean blue, rays from the sun blasted over the witches below. Their skin started to liquify, bubbling as it fell off in slimy tufts like Zula's fur. One by one they melted into individual piles of putrid mush on the ground, screaming into the sun as they dissolved into brown smelly slime. I stood in the circle of flames, bleeding, guts hanging out, and laughing maniacally into the daylight.

Stella crawled toward me with her disintegrating body, limbs hanging from gooey threads before dissolving into black dust. My face was wet with tears watching the girl I loved crumble into rotten emptiness, but still I cradled the bag of herbs in my aching hand, the other tightly bound against my molten weapon.

"Was it all fake?" I sobbed, hoping for a moment things would all go back to normal. That Stella's face would return to its perfect roundness, that her soft supple cheeks would beam when she smiled. But her face still melted off their bones, ripping into shreds, and oozing as it burned. "Even when we were kids?"

"No ..." Stella croaked; her vocal cords shriveling the more she spoke. "My uncle ... taught me ... he was all I ... had. I loved ... you ... Frankie ..."

With one last huff, she fainted into the snow.

"I guess this is goodbye," I said to Stella's withering face. "Again."

My mother must have slipped away into the smoke from the fire, now nowhere to be found. But regardless of the sun beating on my pounding head, the night was still not over.

I knew she'd be back, one way or another.

I was finally alone ... but not for long.

BURN THE WITCH

"I won again, Mama!" I screamed at the warming sun, soft flurries of snow wisping by. Sankta Lucia candles flickered behind my eyes, glowing like the burning star above. "Aren't you proud of me?"

Cackling like a crow into the sunny blue sky, coughing up bits of phlegm and chunks of bloody guts, I waited patiently for her return, the holes in my legs and side oozing green infection and soot. The wounds warmed to a proper stinging, and then to a burning, but clenching my teeth to relieve the pain, I was almost stoic. The melted piles of ex Kolbe townsfolk rotted into the glowing orange sun, surrounding my trembling feet as I stood in the center of the fire, waiting.

I waited for seconds that turned into minutes, feeling like hours in the bright cold mountains. The peaks of the Babias faded from bloody red to a soft morning pink, inviting the birds and other wildlife back to their homes, no longer afraid of the anxious witches spilling their noxious spells into the atmosphere.

After what felt like days, I heard a rustling at my swollen feet. And from the raging circle of flames, a fiery hand grabbed at my sore ankles, branding black fingerprints into my skin. Her burning body crawled up to mine, throwing her dislocated limbs over my shoulders. Her crooked fingers latched onto my head, stroking my hair like when I was a child. Speaking through her dying voice box, her jaw loose and hanging from the hinges, she vowed to make one last attempt at sucking me back in.

"Remember all the fun we used to have, Franciska?" Her eyes changed from glowing red to their auburn, softening as she spoke to me like the loving mother she'd once pretended to be. "Remember all the nights we spent laughing in your bed, reading a silly book and staying up past your bedtime? I still have the glow in the dark stars stuck to your bedroom ceiling, the ones we put up together when you were just a little girl. Do you remember that? Because I do. I'll always remember that, Franciska. Because you're my only daughter, my only lifeline. Without you, I'm nothing, nothing at all. *I'll die without you.*"

She sobbed crimson tears as I stared at her, unsure what to say or do or feel. My whole life was spent doing things for my mother, making sure it was done her way and to her liking. My own life never truly existed, until I left for the city and promised to never look back. But guilt over leaving my mother had only ever gotten me as far as winding back up in her trap. The shame she instilled in me raised me to be a people pleaser, a pushover, a good-for-nothing wimp who hated the world and everything in it. I couldn't escape this cycle of shame and guilt if she was still around.

With tears stinging the cuts that overtook my swollen face, I wrapped myself around my mother, squeezing her tightly into me, my blood mixing with hers. I held her for a moment, the both of us sobbing into each other, holding each other tightly. Like a perfect family unit, we embraced for the final time, like the closure we'd never gotten when I ran away to the city. For the first time since the day I was born, I think we finally started to understand each other.

Grabbing a pile of herbs and petals that fell to the fire, I poured them over her melting head, blessing her one last time.

"Poppy petals for sleep and unease, Mama."

The shard of molten metal went into her back like a knife in room temperature butter, ripping through her meat and gushing buckets of blood and guts and black sludge, spilling onto the ground and oozing into the fire.

The second blow went to her neck, slicing open her jugular.

The third and fourth swipes were quite erratic, my hands stabbing into flesh I couldn't even see in my fury.

I counted forty-five repeated stabbing motions before I got to her heart. The metal shard broke in half once it slipped past her ribs, metal splinters making their way into her cavities. Her chest opened wide, pouring out black and purple guck and piles of smelly worms that slithered away before melting into the earth. Rancid gasses released from her orifices and raised to the sky, covering the mountains in a thick black smog.

Attempting to stand on my throbbing legs was like getting on splintering stilts—they cracked and wobbled and stung with pain that shot up my legs, into my back, and beyond. A scream formed in the deepest pit of my gut, and I let it thrash and rage through my scratchy throat so the whole world could hear me. The birds who were once singing their morning songs shut their beaks letting me scream into the air. Screaming until I fabricated enough strength, I finally stood up on my broken legs, grasping my mother by her stringy hair. I dragged her through the mud and soot, through the snow and ice and finally through the fire to the edge of the Babias, giving her a kiss on her gooey forehead before letting go.

"It's over, Mom."

With just a little flick on her forehead I toppled her over the blue mountaintops. She spun in fiery circles as she tumbled down to the dirt, thousands and thousands of miles below. Torn off arms and legs slid down the slippery snow, fading away in the vast valleys hidden deep beneath. Her screams infiltrated the air as she flew further and further into the distance, howling at the invisible moon. Her earth-shattering wails haunted me as they got further and further away, until they sounded like whispers in the wind.

I watched until she disappeared, a lost speck of nothing in the mountaintops. And then I collapsed.

Into the mountains ...

I ... will ... fall ...

The hills were thick with pine trees and brush, snow blanketing my exposed feet and soothing the burns on my ankles. I crawled for miles down the rocky Babia mountains, watching the sun rise even higher as I made my way down, following a golden light in the distance.

A hundred feet from my destination, I found solace in an old building standing tall in the distance. The glowing Kolbe church, where all of the night's festivities had started, looked glorious now that it was my only salvation. But the closer I got to the door, I collapsed again, my legs no longer able to handle the weight of my aching body. I used what little I had left inside my chest to call toward the church's giant wooden doors, until they swung open, and an elderly man came limping toward me.

The white light of the snow around me clouded my vision, circles of glittery light forming in my eyes, until they disappeared, and the world was black again.

FESTIVAL OF LIGHTS

DECEMBER 13TH

Warm water trickled under my chin, soft cloth gracing the skin on my cheeks. A soothing warmth washed over my body that laid on soft cushions, supporting my back. My eyes opened slowly, blurred glimmers of orange light seeping through the cracks in my eyelids. A friendly looking elderly man, at least in his nineties, was rubbing my face gently with a warm washcloth, and my legs were wrapped in white bandages. soaked already by blood.

"She lives!" The man exclaimed, noticing my consciousness resume. His face was familiar but distant, like I'd known him from the past or had seen him in my dreams. When his eyes opened wider, checking to see if there were any gears turning behind my sockets, the hazel of his irises jogged my memory. "Franciska, are you there?"

I slithered back, not knowing if this was a dream or a continuation of my very real nightmares. The old man from the diner, the one who attacked me at the table, warning me not to go to the feast, was nursing my wound as we were surrounded by tiny red votives burning hundreds of white candles around us. I looked up and saw the stained glass of the church; sheltered inside again.

"Who ... who are you?" I uttered.

"Don't be scared. I'm only here to help."

"How do you know my name?"

"I've known you since you were a girl, Franciska. But I'm sure you don't remember all those years ago. My name is Father Adamik, I'm the Bishop here at the Kolbe Church."

"I do remember you!" I coughed, exerting too much energy and being forced to lay back down on my matted hair. "But I saw you the other night. You ... you were looking at me through the windows. You tried to warn me. At least I think that was you ..."

"Yes, that was me. I apologize if my staring frightened you. I saw you come into the diner with that woman ... and something gave me urgency. I felt compelled to protect you somehow. But I wasn't sure how to approach you with no evidence other than this aching gut feeling that just wouldn't go away. So, I suppose I just ... watched over you."

"What? You never came into the diner? But I saw you! I saw—"

"Shh, my child. You must try to rest. It's all behind us now."

"What's behind us?'

"The feast ... all of it."

"But won't this change things? Won't the townspeople be upset?"

"Our joy doesn't come from the feast, nor the darkness that plagued this town hundreds of years ago. It comes from our traditions, the ones that hold us together when evil tries to destroy us. Our joy comes from the festival of lights, from *Sankta Lucia*. And if you listen closely, you may begin to hear the celebration starting. It's not too late, Franciska. Just listen to the music ..."

Organs played proudly from afar, behind the closed doors of whatever glowing room the priest had taken me to in my illness. My heart purred, listening to the music that played out in the sanctuary and beyond the four walls of my confines. Footsteps increased as unseen people rushed into the church, and the crack under the door revealed more glowing light shining through. I closed my eyes, allowing the voices to carry me through my pain.

Hark! Through the darksome night,
Sounds come a winging.
Lo! Tis the Queen of Light,
Joyfully singing.
Clad in her garment white,
Wearing her crown of light.
Sankta Lucia,
Sankta Lucia.

The next morning, I awoke to tubes connected to my chest and plastic lines stuck into the veins in my arms. Fluorescent lights beamed into my waking eyes, burning the bandaged wounds on my body. Machines beeped all around me, indicating signs of life. A sterile hospital was a welcomed treat after the night I'd had.

"She awakens!" Father Adamik sat in a plastic chair in the corner of the room, shuffling through a newspaper that read *December 14th, 1995*. I'd lost a whole day in the confines of my hospital bed. "How are you feeling, my child?"

He pulled a piece of saffron bread from his pocket, wrapped in a napkin that I could only assume he saved from the day before at the celebration I'd missed. Placing his hand on my forehead, he blessed me without words.

"I remember you, father," I said softly, my throat sore and scratchy. "And not just from the other night, but from before. You saved me, as a kid. My mother was trying to—"

"*Shhh*, my child," he said, wiping the saffron breadcrumbs from my chin. "Now is the time for rest."

I ate my bread in silence as the old priest read his newspaper over a hundred times, until visiting hours were over, and it was time for him to leave.

I stopped him as he was putting on his dark wool coat, ready for the bustling winter outside the hospital doors. There was only one more thing I needed to say.

"I found that old pouch of herbs in my mom's house. The one you gave me all those years ago." I laughed under my breath, finding the words silly but still important to say. "I kept it in my pocket since the day I found it, I didn't know what it was for, but it felt … necessary."

"Do you still have the pouch, my girl?" His eyes bulged as he took his hat from his head and held it at his side, leaning on the plastic bed rails. "I'd like to see it, maybe even bless it again if you don't mind."

"Oh," I said, looking around my hospital room as if I was going to find anything in the sea of sterile white. "I think I may have lost it in the mountains or maybe when I fell at your door …"

The old priest's hands trembled, his lips pinching into a thin sliver of wrinkled nothing. His skin turned a pale pink, washing away with the burning of the fluorescents.

"That's … unfortunate," he said, voice shaking. "I'm sorry, Franciska, but I must be leaving now. Please take care, will you?"

"Wait," I stopped him again, "is something wrong?"

"Oh, no," he forced out of his wobbly throat, looking down to avoid suspicion of an obvious lie. "The herbs are just an old Polish tradition—an old wives' tale, if you will. Silly as it is, I thought … I thought maybe they'd protect you. But I'm sure it'll all be fine. Surely, you'll be leaving here soon, anyway."

The fluorescents flickered green and yellow as he walked away, buzzing like bees until they burnt out completely. Alone again and in the dark once more, if I listened closely, I could still hear the faint cackling of witches, screaming their spells to the bloody moon.

EPILOGUE

Months later, I was released from the Kolbe County hospital after healing as much as possible from my injuries. Crutches were a necessary mobility aid for the foreseeable future, but I was alive and as well as I could be, all things considered.

The magazine sent flowers and cards to my hospital bed for weeks after I'd been admitted, promising that my job was waiting for me when I felt better. But I phoned my secretary a few days after the incident, letting her know to put in my resignation. I couldn't imagine ever feeling healthy enough to spend my days trying to please my boss ever again.

Father Adamik promised to take care of Zula for me, vowing never to let her out of any cracked windows, avoiding another opossum situation. I'd like to imagine they found solace in each other, two elderly companions living out their last days together, until their bodies slowed to their timely deaths—having lived long and fruitful lives.

The taxi dropped me off in front of my mother's house, decrepit and falling apart. My Bronco looked disheveled with flat tires and broken windows, piles of snow inside the driver's seat. It must have taken quite a blow sitting there in the driveway when the storms hit, wreaking havoc on the town. I decided to let it rot there.

I stepped inside the crumbling house, soaking in the sunshine that forced its way through the crack in the kitchen window, illuminating the place and revealing the piles of dust and grime that had accumulated over the years. I gathered my things quickly, knowing the cab driver outside was waiting on the clock to take me to the airport hours away, a steep tip awaiting him.

But as I was saying my goodbyes to the house and the memories of my childhood, something felt strange. My mother's presence was still thick in the musty air and not just because of all her things that inhabited the home. Her energy still existed, swirling around me like flies in a dumpster.

In a flash the fireplace ignited, roaring flames through the living room.

A burning body crawled through the hole in the wall, bones cracking and twisting in unnatural ways.

Sharp teeth oozed green foam, salivating at my scent.

She came closer, and closer, and closer, until she was centimeters from my face.

"As long as you're alive," she screeched, "I'll always have something to feed on!"

I put my hands out in defense, attempting to back away but cornered by more fire seeping into the walls and floor below me. I backed up until the flames engulfed me, and her jaw opened wider than my body, revealing the millions of stabbing rotting teeth waiting to eat me up.

"MAMA NO!!!!!"

ACKNOWLEDGEMENTS

I feel compelled to start this by saying that this book sort of fell into my lap. It was born from a failed attempt at another witchy mother story that I had tried to get published elsewhere, with no luck. When I decided to turn it into a novella, I thought I was just going to be taking the same story and simply making it longer, so it didn't feel as rushed as it had previously. But when I started to plan out the rewrites, it dawned on me that the story I wanted to tell was a little bit different.

Growing up as a Polish-Irish-American kid from the north side of Chicago, I was immersed with tons of culture. But more specifically, I was raised in a Swedish neighborhood (that's also, ironically, known as an incredibly Queer neighborhood.) My mom also happened to work at the local Swedish Lutheran Church, and I had spent many a Saint Lucia Day watching the girls with their crowns of candles proceed into the dark cathedral. I thought I was the only non-Swedish person who had ever heard of it.

So when I found out that there was Polish folklore surrounding the festival of lights—that the culture I was born into oddly mixed with the culture of my childhood surroundings—I knew that was my story. They say that you should write what you know, and in this case, the things that I "knew" were waiting for me the entire time. Diving into research about The Night of the Witches was not only fun for me but felt like some sort of sign from the universe that everything was going to fall into place. There was never a doubt that this is what Feeding Lucy had to be about.

That's not to say, however, that writing this book didn't come without its challenges. The story may have fallen into my lap, but the writing of it didn't. The characters were a mess, I was holding back on what I really wanted to say, and I couldn't get out of my own damn head. There were times that I didn't think I'd get to see an end product at all. But after rewriting the protagonist to fit the narrative I wanted, forcing myself through several rewrites, revisions, and edits, and buckets of sweat and tears, I finally had something I was proud of. I had a totally Sapphic, Witchy Folk Horror that combined two worlds that previously only existed in my life simultaneously.

But I don't think I could've done this by myself (at least not without losing my sanity.) The people who helped make this story a reality are some of the most talented people I have ever met, and I couldn't be prouder to say that they were with me throughout the process of creating this silly little book.

Before anyone else, I have to give a shout out to my daughter, Anastasja, who helped keep me sane as I attempted on many occasions to rip the hairs from my head one by one. Her knowledge of healthy coping tools really helped me breathe a bit easier when things got ... frustrating. Being a mother is hard, but it makes it easier with a kid like her.

Speaking of mothers, I can't forget my own. My ma' not only raised me to be the bull-headed Chicagoan that I am, but I inherited some of those witchy ways of hers, which helped pull me into the heart of this story. She's also the reason for the name Ostrowski, her maiden name and unfortunately one that I've never had as my own, but always felt connected to.

I dedicated this book to (and named a character after) my great grandmother, Stanisława, or "Stella"—even though I'd never met her—because I didn't want her story to end where it did. She deserves to have a piece of her live in everything that I do.

And none of this would have been possible if it weren't for the little neighborhood of Andersonville in Chicago where I grew up. Nor would any of it make sense if I hadn't spent all those years hiding in the "ghost attic" of Ebenezer Lutheran Church, where I first learned about Sankta Lucia and where I told my friends many a ghost (or monster, or creepy murderer ...) story. Sure, I could have done my research and written it even without the lived experience of having watched this event in person, but I think it would lose a little of its authenticity.

So even though I'm not religious in my real life, I appreciate those moments in time for how they shaped me and my writing.

But beyond taking bits and pieces from the life I've lived and the things I've picked up along the way, there's people who in real-time helped Lucy physically come alive.

First I have to thank my unofficial (yet totally official) critique partner, David Washburn. Not only did he quite literally name the book, but he was along for the ride from the first rejected iteration of the story to the final result that it's become. His advice and encouragement carried me through to the end, even when I thought I wouldn't write ever again (and yes, I know I'm dramatic.)

My beta readers were a huge help in moving this thing along, too. They showed me all the holes in the original story, were honest when they didn't like something, and are inadvertently the reason I made such a big change by rewriting my protagonist. Without them, I'm not sure I would've ever seen what wasn't working.

And when talking about fixing holes and polishing a messy story, I couldn't forget my editor, Nico Bell. Their thoroughness and care with my manuscript made it better than it could've ever been with just goofy ol' me editing it. I'm so thankful for their hard work on Lucy and I promise as a reader you will thank me for hiring them. (Oh, and I found out I don't know how to use a semicolon. So double thank me for hiring Nico.)

Christy Aldridge at Grim Poppy Designs is another huge part of this whole process, creating an amazing cover that exceeded my expectations. She took an inspo pic, a vague idea, and a (really convoluted) description of the story, and made a cover that's so beautifully creepy I haven't stopped staring at it for months. Lucy is deliciously ferocious and I'm so thankful for Christy for her talent.

And I can't forget to thank Joey Powell at Mad Axe Media, who is the whole reason anyone is even reading this without throwing it in the fire for being too ugly or hard to read. I couldn't have formatted this thing myself, that's for sure.

I'm forever grateful to Joey for making the inside of my book just as beautiful as the outside.

In general, the indie horror community is the catalyst for all of these friends and collaborators I've been so lucky to have met over the years. It isn't a coincidence I ended up where I did, and I'm just grateful it exists as a safe place to be myself.

And although I'd never met him, I'd be remiss to not thank Hunter S. Thompson for creating this monster inside me. Gonzo was burned into my blood at a young age, and I don't think I'd ever write the same if it weren't for him. I will *always* put myself into the narrative, even if nobody knows it but me.

And lastly, I have to thank the readers. I'd be a fool to think any of this could happen without you. All I've ever wanted was people to read the stories that come from my chaotic brain, so thank you all for sticking around and fueling my hunger to write more. Without you, I'd just be a weird gremlin in my hidey-hole, writing words on paper that would never get read by anyone but me. So thank you, from the bottom of my little black heart.

ABOUT THE AUTHOR

Mo Medusa is a Queer and Disabled Writer, Vocalist, and Fiction Writing Mentor from Chicago, IL. Their current focus is on Horror Fiction, Literary Fiction, Creative Nonfiction, and Poetry. In their spare time, they enjoy deep diving into new music finds, sipping a (non-alcoholic) beer by the lake, and watching way too much trash TV. Mo lives on the north side with their cats, birds, and human child.

STAY CONNECTED WITH MO MEDUSA

momedusa.com

Instagram | Facebook | Threads

@momedusahorror